BARELY

HEARD

(A Tessa Flint FBI Suspense Thriller —Book 2)

Molly Black

Molly Black

Bestselling author Molly Black is author of the MAYA GRAY FBI suspense thriller series, comprising ten books (and counting); of the RYLIE WOLF FBI suspense thriller series, comprising six books; of the TAYLOR SAGE FBI suspense thriller series, comprising eight books; of the KATIE WINTER FBI suspense thriller series, comprising eleven books (and counting); of the RUBY HUNTER FBI suspense thriller series, comprising five books (and counting); of the CAITLIN DARE FBI suspense thriller series, comprising six books (and counting); of the REESE LINK mystery series, comprising six books (and counting); of the CLAIRE KING FBI suspense thriller series, comprising seven books (and counting); of the PIPER WOODS mystery series, comprising five books (and counting); of the GRACE FORD mystery series, comprising seven books (and counting); of the CASEY BOLT mystery series, comprising five books (and counting); of the JADE SAVAGE mystery series, comprising five books (and counting); and of the TESSA FLINT mystery series, comprising five books (and counting).

An avid reader and lifelong fan of the mystery and thriller genres, Molly loves to hear from you, so please feel free to visit www.mollyblackauthor.com to learn more and stay in touch.

ISBN:978-1-0943-9728-3

BOOKS BY MOLLY BLACK

TESSA FLINT MYSTERY SERIES
BARELY SEEN (Book #1)
BARELY HEARD (Book #2)
BARELY FORGOTTEN (Book #3)
BARELY MISSING (Book #4)
BARELY ALIVE (Book #5)

JADE SAVAGE MYSTERY SERIES
ALL SHE FEARS (Book #1)
ALL SHE WANTS (Book #2)
ALL SHE REMEMBERS (Book #3)
ALL SHE NEEDS (Book #4)
ALL SHE HIDES (Book #5)

CASEY BOLT MYSTERY SERIES
BROKEN (Book #1)
FLAWED (Book #2)
BLEMISHED (Book #3)
DAMAGED (Book #4)
TWISTED (Book #5)

GRACE FORD MYSTERY SERIES
NEARLY MINE (Book #1)
NEARLY SAFE (Book #2)
NEARLY FREE (Book #3)
NEARLY GONE (Book #4)
NEARLY HIS (Book #5)

CLAIRE KING MYSTERY SERIES
ONCE HE SEES (Book #1)
ONCE HE LONGS (Book #2)
ONCE HE TAKES (Book #3)
ONCE HE FEELS (Book #4)

ONCE HE KNOWS (Book #5)

MAYA GRAY MYSTERY SERIES
GIRL ONE: MURDER (Book #1)
GIRL TWO: TAKEN (Book #2)
GIRL THREE: TRAPPED (Book #3)
GIRL FOUR: LURED (Book #4)
GIRL FIVE: BOUND (Book #5)
GIRL SIX: FORSAKEN (Book #6)
GIRL SEVEN: CRAVED (Book #7)
GIRL EIGHT: HUNTED (Book #8)
GIRL NINE: GONE (Book #9)

RYLIE WOLF FBI SUSPENSE THRILLER
FOUND YOU (Book #1)
CAUGHT YOU (Book #2)
SEE YOU (Book #3)
WANT YOU (Book #4)
TAKE YOU (Book #5)
DARE YOU (Book #6)

TAYLOR SAGE FBI SUSPENSE THRILLER
DON'T LOOK (Book #1)
DON'T BREATHE (Book #2)
DON'T RUN (Book #3)
DON'T FLINCH (Book #4)
DON'T REMEMBER (Book #5)
DON'T TELL (Book #6)

KATIE WINTER FBI SUSPENSE THRILLER
SAVE ME (Book #1)
REACH ME (Book #2)
HIDE ME (Book #3)
BELIEVE ME (Book #4)
HELP ME (Book #5)
FORGET ME (Book #6)
HOLD ME (Book #7)
PROTECT ME (Book #8)
REMEMBER ME (Book #9)
CATCH ME (Book #10)

WATCH ME (Book #11)

RUBY HUNTER FBI SUSPENSE THRILLER
IF I RUN (Book #1)
IF I TELL (Book #2)
IF I LIVE (Book #3)
IF I FORGET (Book #4)
IF I RETURN (Book #5)

CAITLIN DARE FBI SUSPENSE THRILLER
COME GET ME (Book #1)
COME FIND ME (Book #2)
COME TAKE ME (Book #3)
COME CATCH ME (Book #4)
COME SAVE ME (Book #5)

REESE LINK MYSTERY
BEYOND REASON (Book #1)
BEYOND REACH (Book #2)
BEYOND REPAIR (Book #3)
BEYOND DOUBT (Book #4)
BEYOND NORMAL (Book #5)

PROLOGUE

The frigid air bit at Rachel's cheeks as she carved her way down the mountain, twin trails of powder marking her descent. The moon cast an ethereal glow over the private ski slope that had become her go-to location for burning off some stress. This was where she felt alive – away from the clamor of competitive circuits and the weight of expectations – where she could hone her craft on her own terms.

Rachel Coolidge leaned into the turn, her snowboard responding instantly, edges biting into the hard-packed snow with guided precision. The sound of her heartbeat thrummed in her ears, merging with the hiss of her board slicing through the night. And she was the only one out here, all alone on this perfect slope. Of course, she had to pay a hefty price for such a privilege, but it was worth it. She relished the solitude, the way the shadows played across the snow-covered pines, creating an illusion of movement where there was none.

She pushed herself faster, welcoming the rush, the sense of teetering on the edge of control. It was a familiar intoxication, one that had driven her ever since she first strapped into a board at six years old, propelled by an insatiable hunger for speed and the thrill of competition.

The slope ahead was steep, a tempting challenge, and she accepted it without hesitation. Dropping low, she became a blur against the canvas of white and darkness, each breath forming a fleeting cloud that lingered behind her. Her muscles tensed and relaxed in a practiced cadence, honed from years of competition and the relentless pursuit of perfection.

But tonight was not about medals or accolades; it was just Rachel and the mountain, two old friends catching up. The descent was nearing its end, the base of the slope approaching too quickly for her liking. She figured she could do gown one more time but after that, she'd have to stop. She needed to rest her knees and ankles. There was an upcoming competition to think of, after all. Plus, it was getting late, the clock inching closer to midnight.

When the run came to an end, she stood at the bottom of the slope and looked back up with a smile. She'd mastered this run years ago, but the familiarity of it always made her appreciative of how far she'd come in her career. She's started on the small slopes at Sugarloaf and now, at the age of twenty-four, knew all of the slopes and runs at that famous Maine ski resort like the back of her hand—the ones over at Sunday River, too. So when she' been able to afford it, she'd sought out these private, more challenging runs that…

Her concentration snapped when she noticed the faint, silver glint coming from one of the spruce trees to her right. There, where the run ended, there was a safety wall installed directly in front of a massive grove of spruce trees. Her eyes still on that strange sparkle coming from the trees, Rachel slowly unclasped her feet free of her snowboard. She walked over to the spruces, wary and curious.

And then her curiosity shifted into something else—a restless unease that caused her to go still for a moment.

There was a snowflake-shaped pendant dangling from the crisp, green branch of the spruce closest to the protective wall. The silver pendant hung from a silver chain, spinning slowly, catching the silver moonlight.

The pendant struck a tiny chord of fear in her heart because it eerily similar to the one she had received in the mail several weeks ago. In fact, as she drew closer to it and studied it, she saw that it was *identical* to that pendant.

The one she'd received in the mail had been wrapped in anonymity and accompanied by words of admiration scrawled on a plain card. That pendant lay secure in her locker back at the small gym at home, yet here swung its twin, as if conjured by the mountain itself.

She reached out to take it, her fingertips grazing the metal; it felt almost like a silent summons, a lure to draw her in.

The intricate patterns etched into the pendant's surface were identical to her own—a signature of sorts, she had thought at first, a mark of an admirer who knew her taste or perhaps knew her too well. She allowed herself a moment of contemplation, her instincts whispering insidiously that this was no mere coincidence. The quietude around her now held a weight, as if charged with an expectation of something yet to unfold.

Her gaze shifted from the pendant to the surrounding woods, her ears straining for any sound that might penetrate the stillness. But there was nothing –only the occasional creak of aged timber and the soft sigh of the breeze through the needles. Unease coiled in her gut, a primal alertness that made her skin prickle beneath the layers of thermal fabric.

"Who's there?" The question emerged as a whisper, more to herself than anyone else.

There was no response, only her own breath forming clouds that dissipated quickly in the night air.

A chill that had nothing to do with the mountain's frosty air crept down Rachel's spine. No longer interested in that final run down the course, she turned, grabbed her board, and started back for the small cabin that guests used to change and get warm. But it was there, just at the edge of the cabin's grounds, that she spotted a figure. They were wearing a puffy coat, ski pants, and a ski mask. The mask itself was unremarkable, a familiar sight to those who spent a lot of time in the snow. But it was the stillness of the person behind it, the way they seemed to blend seamlessly with the shadows, that unnerved her.

Rachel's breath hitched, frozen fog hanging before her like a whisper of alarm. She wasn't prone to fear; the slopes were her domain, and yet this silent observer managed to evoke an instinctual response—a pang of fear that resonated deep in her core. The athletic grace that served her so well on a snowboard felt suddenly like a traitor's gift, her muscles tensing for action when her mind screamed for caution.

"Can I help you?" she called out, her voice steadier than she felt.

The figure made no move, offered no response, merely stood watchful and enigmatic. With each passing second, the quiet grew heavier, pressing against her with all the subtlety of a threat left unspoken.

Forcing a laugh to mask the tremor of unease, Rachel continued for the cabin. It was probably just another tourist, she reasoned, someone with a lot of money who wanted an unparalleled skiing or boarding experience.

But this late? she wondered. *And besides, I had the slot booked. No one else should be here.*

As she took another step forward, the realization dawned with chilling clarity—the figure had moved, imperceptibly but deliberately, blocking her path to the front door.

"Excuse me," Rachel said, her tone now edged with the sharpness of adrenaline. She kept her gaze fixed on the darkened eye slits of the ski mask, searching for some hint, some glimpse into the figure's intentions.

With a practiced calm born of countless competitions, Rachel weighed her options. Confrontation was a gamble, escape might provoke pursuit, and stalling could be just as dangerous.

"Look, if you need help, I can call ski patrol," she proposed, reaching for her phone with hands that betrayed none of her inner turmoil. The figure shifted, a subtle coiling of posture that spoke volumes to Rachel's heightened senses. They were now roughly fifteen feet apart, and that suddenly felt *far* too close.

Rachel's instincts screamed at her to move. He might be blocking the cabin, but she had the relative safety of the spruces behind her. And if she really needed to, she could run up the now-immobile belt that carried skiers and boarders the top of the run. And when she reached the top, she could hop on her board and run down the side; it wasn't an actual run but she'd done it a few times before on dares, just for a bit of fun. That would bring her to the edge of the parking lot. And once she was on her board, there was no way this creep would catch her.

With a surge of adrenaline, she pivoted and ran for the edge of the course. She ran with her snowboard tucked under her arm, and for a moment it felt like a shield.

She glanced over her shoulder and saw that the figure was in pursuit, moving with an eerie, silent grace that belied the bulkiness of the ski gear. Panic clawed at Rachel's throat, and she propelled herself forward with desperate energy, carving a frantic path forward. The belt platform was just ahead of her, to the far left side of the slope, bordered by even more spruces.

"Help! Somebody help me!" she cried out. But the vast expanse of white around her absorbed the sound, leaving her pleas as nothing more than whispers lost to the wilderness. There was no one around, no hope of a passing skier or late-night patrol. It was just her and the masked figure, a deadly chase under an uncaring moon.

Another look back told her that the figure was gaining ground. They were fast and also not incumbered by carrying a snowboard. But Rachel knew that if she diched her board, she'd be helpless when she finally reached the top. Her board was the entire key to this escape. She was also vaguely aware that her fear made her movements jerky, uncoordinated.

The belt platform was there, just ten feet away. She eyed it climbing up the slope, the night sky nothing more than a void at the top. She let out a moan of desperation as she ran for it, hating that she was *this* scared.

It was then that a weight crashed down upon her, driving the breath from her lungs. She hit the ground hard. Snow filled her mouth, her nostrils, suffocatingly soft but as deadly as concrete. She fought against the oppressive force, her muscles screaming in protest, her fingers clawing for purchase in the deceptive powder.

"Get off me!" Rachel's muffled shout was barely audible as the figure pressed down harder. Her vision started to dim, the edges of her sight encroaching with creeping darkness. All her strength, all her determination, seemed pitifully futile against this assailant who wielded the very mountain against her. The snow burned her cheeks filled her mouth, scaling down her throat in a cold, jagged sheet.

His force was relentless, the pressure unyielding. This was no random encounter; the figure had sought her out, had waited for her in the shadows with malevolent intent. *But why?*

There was no time to find an answer. Her body began to betray her, limbs heavy as lead, each movement an immense effort that yielded little. The cold seeped into her bones, a paralyzing sensation she'd only glimpsed before, but it was now engulfing her.

Her last thought before the darkness took her in its cold grip was the pendant. Was this the fan who had sent it to her? And if so, why had they decided to turn such a symbol sinister?

Before she could focus on it, the darkness grabbed her and pulled her down in a fit of spasming lungs and a frigid, black nothing.

CHAPTER ONE

Tessa's fists cut through the air with precision, her sweat-slicked skin reflecting the dim overhead lights of the bureau gym. The rhythmic thud of gloves against pads punctuated each strike as she danced around Jake, who was holding the kickboxing mitts. Her breath came in controlled bursts, her muscles tight and poised for the next strike.

"Come on, Tessa, hit like you mean it," Jake teased, his grin wide beneath the protective headgear.

She responded not with words but with a flurry of jabs and a roundhouse kick that made him stagger back a step, despite his solid frame. Each strike against the pads sounded like a small explosion within the confines of the bureau gymnasium. Tessa didn't feel the impact reverberate up her shin, but she saw the acknowledgment in Jake's eyes. It was as if her body moved with a mind of its own, honed by years of training to compensate for her inability to sense physical pain.

The gym wasn't her favorite place by any means, but it was often a great precursor to days upon days of fieldwork—an expanse of rubber mats and hanging bags where agents purged their stress in sweat. She and Jake had been meeting once a week, an hour before work, to get out some aggression out and hone their skills—while also bonding tighter as partners.

A jab-cross combo followed by a swift uppercut sent the mitts clapping loudly. Tessa felt a surge of satisfaction at the perfect execution of technique, knowing well the balance between control and aggression.

"Oof! That'll bruise," Jake conceded, momentarily dropping his guard to rub at the spot Tessa had targeted. His pained expression was exaggerated, playing it up for effect—just another tease designed to elicit a chuckle or at least a smirk from his partner.

Their sparring slowed, transitioning from aggressive combat to a playful dance of feints and dodges. Jake's outgoing nature surfaced in his chuckles and light-hearted quips, parries that were met with Tessa's quiet tenacity. They circled each other on the mat, partners in a ballet of disciplined movement. Every now and then, though, she'd see his eyes light up with surprise at the power behind a strike.

"Ever consider pulling your punches?" Jake asked, his voice teasing, though his eyes were attentive to her every move.

"Only when I'm up against overconfident partners," Tessa shot back, her lips twitching with the ghost of a smile.

"Ouch," Jake said, pretending to clutch his heart. "You wound me, Flint."

Their banter was a familiar rhythm, as integral to their routine as the workouts themselves. It bridged the gap between their contrasting personalities, creating a camaraderie that had seen them through countless cases and near misses. With Jake, Tessa could almost forget the loneliness her condition often imposed upon her.

"Better wounded pride than wounded in the line of duty," she retorted, sending a quick sidekick in his direction that he narrowly dodged.

"True enough," he conceded, stepping back and lowering his mitts. Tessa mirrored his movements, the two of them coming to a natural pause. The echo of their exertions lingered, blending with the distant sound of weights being racked elsewhere in the bureau's fitness center.

As their time came to a close, both due at the morning's briefing in just twenty minutes, Tessa unsheathed her fists from the gloves, the velcro tearing away with a sound that sliced through the lingering tension. She rolled her shoulders back, feeling the pull of exertion but not the ache—a reminder of her condition—while Jake mirrored her, wincing as he did so. She knew that when the day came to a close, she'd find torn skin on her knuckles, something that may cause a sting or irritation for others. But for her, it was nothing. She'd often tear the skin on her knuckles during these sessions and not even know it until she removed the gloves and found that she'd bed into them.

She and Jake settled onto the mat, cross-legged and facing each other, their breaths evening out as they each took a long gulp from their water bottles. Jake wiped his brow with the back of his hand, still catching his breath. Tessa watched him from the corner of her eye, something she'd found herself doing quite a bit lately. She wouldn't say she'd started to develop a crush on Jake, but there was *something* there…something she wasn't ready to face just yet. Mainly because she had no idea where it had come from.

And maybe it was those feelings that made it surprisingly easy to speak the words that started to come out of her mouth, much to her surprise.

"Listen," Tessa began, her voice quieter now, "I've been thinking about Sarah's case again."

Jake's expression sobered instantly. He knew all too well the unresolved ache of Tessa's past, the sister whose death remained cloaked in mystery. And he seemed both awkward and warm whenever Sarah's name was mentioned.

"Thinking *what*, exactly?

"Thinking of submitting an official request to Lawson to get the case opened again."

Jake thought about it for a moment, sipping water. "That's going to be a tough nut to crack, Tess. A cold case with a personal connection? Good luck."

"I just need to find a new angle, something the original investigators missed," she murmured, her fingers tracing the condensation on her bottle. The notion of reopening such a personal case was daunting, yet the persistent coil of unanswered questions left her no peace.

"Hey," Jake said gently, reaching over to give her shoulder a squeeze—a gesture filled with unspoken support. "If you want to go down that road, I've got your back. You know that, right?"

"I know." Tessa offered him a soft, grateful smile.

The touching moment was halted abruptly as the door to the sparring square opened up. Special Agent in Charge Rebecca Lawson strode into the gym, her presence commanding immediate attention. Though it was a bit odd to see Lawson in the gym, Tessa knew she must be here for something important to make such an appearance. She was the sort of leader whose reputation preceded her, known for her sharp intellect and sharper instincts. Tessa and Jake both stood, instinctively straightening in front of their superior.

"Flint, Sullivan." Lawson addressed them crisply, her eyes scanning their post-workout dishevelment with approval. "Did you get in a good session?"

"I did, for sure," Jake said. "But Flint here needs work."

Lawson chuffed and shook her head, not buying it for a moment. Her expression then shifted, slipping into all business. "We've received news of a murder near Sunday River. And everything about it is lining up perfectly with another murder out of that general area earlier in the week."

"You mean the ice skater, right?" Tessa said.

"Yes. An ice skater by the name of Elana Dean was killed four days ago. Basic strangulation, and there was a pendant on her neck that no one in her family, including her husband, recognized. And now we have a second…the exact same thing. Only it wasn't an ice skater this time—it was a professional snowboarder by the name of Rachel Coolidge."

Tessa's heart didn't race—she had trained herself to stay calm in any situation—but her thoughts accelerated. Patterns, motives, possibilities…it was already all racing through her mind, constructing and deconstructing scenarios with meticulous precision.

"Any leads?" Jake asked.

"None that stand out yet. But I want you two on it. You handled the last high-profile case with a finesse that's needed here. These ladies weren't exactly famous, but they're well-known enough that if the media gets on it, it could blow up into a much larger case. And we would, of course, like to avoid that."

Lawson's confidence in their abilities was a mantle Tessa accepted without hesitation. She knew Lawson had her worries and reservations about an agent with a condition like hers. In many ways, it was a time bomb just waiting to explode. Also, there were so many accomplished and skilled agents under her watch, so it meant a lot that she was coming to them for such a high-profile case.

"Back-to-back winter athletes," she mused aloud. "He's choosing them intentionally. But why? What's the connection besides the sport?"

"Could be a personal vendetta, some twisted form of envy?" Jake suggested, pacing the length of the mat.

"Maybe," Tessa conceded, "or something more symbolic. We need to dig into their backgrounds, find the common thread."

"Are we sure the pendants are identical?" Tessa asked.

"Not sure. That's one of the many things I need you to figure out."

"Well, then," Lawson said. "Get cleaned up and sort out travel. I need you two in snow country as soon as possible—by lunchtime if possible. I'll make sure everything we have on both murders is emailed to you before you leave."

"Understood," Tessa and Jake said, almost at the same time.

Lawson nodded firmly and took her leave. When she was out of the room, Jake let out a small laugh. "That's two cases in a row dealing with necklaces," he commented. "Looks like we're slowly being molded to fit a certain type of case, don't you think?"

"Seems so," Tessa replied. She wasn't amused by the coincidence, but rather intrigued by the challenge it presented.

"Maybe next time we'll get a hat enthusiast or a shoe fanatic."

"God forbid," Tessa chuckled, shaking her head. The absurdity of their banter was a welcome reprieve, a momentary escape from the grim reality of their work. It was a coping mechanism as much as it was a bond between them—this ability to find humor in the darkest places.

"Seriously, though," Jake said, his tone shifting back to earnestness. "There's got to be a reason for the necklaces. Just like last time, it's a part of the killer's MO, something that gives them satisfaction or fulfills some twisted need."

"Agreed," Tessa replied, her focus narrowing once more on the photographs. "And if we can decipher the significance of the pendant, maybe we can predict their next move."

“I’m going to hit the showers really quick,” Jake said. “Meet me at the car in ten?”

“Absolutely.”

Tessa made her own way to the women's locker room, but despite the warm water she stepped beneath, she was already anticipating the colder climates waiting for them just over two hours away.

She also noticed that she had indeed cracked the skin of her knuckles. The skin was peeled back, bleeding freely. She ran her hand under the water, wondering what the sting of it might feel like.

CHAPTER TWO

The snow crunched under Tessa's boots as she and Jake stepped out of the bureau sedan and onto the yard in front of the cabin. The slopes at to the right, the untouched white expanse broken only by the dark outline of police tape fluttering in the frigid wind. Tessa's breath fogged before her face in the biting cold. The early afternoon sunlight glinted like little flecks of gold in the snow. It was a pristine crime scene, almost eerily so, preserved by an unrelenting freeze that had settled upon northern Maine.

"It's sort of beautiful, right?" Jake asked.

"It is."

It was a startling fact, given why they were here. There was something methodical about this setting, something intentional. She furrowed her brow as she considered the psychological implications of such a choice. The killer could have easily obscured their tracks, yet they chose a tableau that seemed designed for discovery. Was it arrogance or a message? A challenge, perhaps?

Or did he simply not care?

"Let's get to work," she said, her voice steady despite the unsettling thoughts swirling in her mind.

They walked to the cabin, where three policemen were huddled on the porch. Out by the slopes, two more were snapping photographs and speaking indistinctly. As they came to the porch, one of the policemen stepped forward. The badge on his chest identified him as the sheriff. He was tall and thin, his arms rather gangly. He wore a well-trimmed moustache that had gone completely white, matching the years his face showed perfectly. Tessa figured he was nearing sixty.

"Agents?" he asked.

Jake reacted first, showing his badge and ID. "Agents Sullivan and Flint."

"Good to meet you," the sheriff said in a thick Maine accent. "I'm Sheriff Bowen, and damn, I'm glad to see you two. Want to follow me out there and get the run down?" he asked, nodding toward the slopes.

"Please, lead the way," Tessa said.

Bowen led them away from the cabin, over toward the slopes where the other cops were still hard at work. He bypassed the officers, walking slightly around them, and pointed to an area in the snow that showed several indentations. Not too far away—maybe eight or ten feet by Tessa's estimation—was the start of the concrete platform that held a conveyor belt that took people to the top of the slope. Being a smaller, private set of slopes, she supposed this was a substitute for a typical ski lift.

"Her body was found right there," Bowen said, pointing to the shape in the show near the concrete platform. Face down. And not just from a fall; her head was *pushed* down into that snow. The coroner says just based on the state of her throat, she breathed in a lot of snow at the end."

The signs of a struggle were obvious—a scuffle in the snow that painted a story of desperation and violence. Amidst the chaos of disrupted snow, a pattern emerged: footprints leading away from the crime scene toward the tree line. But she also took note of the footsteps that came over from the cabin, bordered with crime scene tape that ran from the cabin to set of thin, steel poles the PD had set up. indicating a chase.

Once again, the idea of a killer striking in an environment that would make finding clues and evidence so much easier settled heavily on her. It struck her as a deliberate choice, this wintery stage upon which their killer had set his macabre play. The cold that could preserve also ran the risk of revealing; every misplaced snowflake an accusatory finger pointing at the perpetrator.

"See here?" Tessa pointed out the deeper impressions to Jake. "The victim fought back, tried to run. And over there—the ones veering off are heavier, more deliberate. Our killer's steps."

The tracks led them to the edge of the spruce-lined forest, where shadows danced between the trees. Tessa felt a prickle of unease; the forest loomed like a silent witness keeping its secrets well-guarded.

"Local PD attempted to follow these," Bowen said. "You're welcome to follow them yourself...they're the ones dead center of the trails. The ones bordering them to both sides are us. But it all becomes a jumbled mess half a mile in."

"What kind of mess?" Tessa asked.

"Snow falling from the trees. Animal tracks. And there's also the fact that it looks like the killer purposefully just ran around a bit, making sure we lost the trail."

"Smart," Tessa murmured, her eyes scanning the chaotic mix. "They knew how to cover their escape." She glanced back at the open slope, feeling a surge of determination. They were dealing with someone who understood the game of cat and mouse all too well.

"The hell of it," Bowen said, "is that the tracks seem to just start out of nowhere just before you get to where you parked your car. They come out of the trees but it all loops back around to that mess where everything gets all muddled up. Just a jumble of wildlife trails and windblown chaos. We've combed through what we could, but it's like the forest swallowed this guy whole."

"The preliminary reports we received said there was security camera footage but it yielded nothing useful," Tessa said. "Do you agree with that?"

"Yeah." Bowen nodded back to the porch and said "there's a single camera up there and another at the back, pointed toward the equipment shed. The one on the porch did catch the bastard coming out of the forest, but it's useless footage. He never gets too close to the porch and besides that, he's wearing a ski-mask."

"The murder itself isn't on the footage?"

"Nope."

"To your knowledge, is the pendant still with forensics?" Jake asked.

"It is. And you're welcome to go have a look yourself, if you want."

"I think we will," Tessa said. "Thank you, Sheriff."

Tessa led the way, following the tracks that led across the bottom of the slope and into the woods. She noted that the footprints were spaced a bit further apart than the ones that had led from the edge of the cabin to the place where Rachel Coolidge had been killed. He'd been in an even bigger hurry to leave the scene.

As soon as they passed beneath the canopy of trees—mostly spruces and cedars—she could tell just how hard it would be to track the prints. Among the thick, intoxicating smell of the trees, the footprints began to become little more than divots in the snow. The snow itself was about four-to-five inches in most places, though there were drifts against some of the trees she guessed might be as much as eight inches deep.

"Snowflakes," she said thoughtfully, "each one unique, yet perfectly symmetrical. It's the ultimate paradox, isn't it? Like the athletes this killer is targeting—striving for flawless performance."

"Perfectionism can breed some serious resentment," Jake added, catching on to her train of thought. "From family, even fans, you know?

"Exactly," Tessa agreed. "It could be envy driving our killer—an outsider wanting to destroy what they can't have or be."

"Or someone from within the community," Jake suggested. "Someone who knows just how much pressure these athletes are under—and how far they'll go to achieve perfection."

Tessa nodded, her gaze intently focusing on the footprints in the snow. "This loop of tracks coming out to the forest…this was an escape route planned in advance," she said, her voice steady despite the gravity of their find. "He didn't just stumble upon this place. He chose it. Knew it. And that means he might come back to it."

Together, they mapped the scene meticulously, each measurement and observation another piece of a puzzle they were determined to solve. The chilling thought that they were walking in the footsteps of a killer was not lost on Tessa, but it only served to sharpen her resolve. She would understand this predator, anticipate him—and ultimately, bring him to justice.

Tessa trudged through the thickening blanket of snow, her boots leaving a determined trail behind her. Each step was methodical, mirroring the precision she attributed to their elusive killer. Jake followed close behind, his breath forming crystalline clouds in the frigid air.

They eventually came to the spot Sheriff Bowen had mentioned. The area was roughly twenty feet wide, making a large circle. She could see deer tracks and what might have been a bobcat. She also saw the indentations form where mounds of snow had fallen from the massive cedar beside them. And among it all, heading in five different directions, there were long, scraping prints—obviously placed by human feet and knees. And, again, as Bowen said, they all dead-ended and looped back around on one another, leading back toward the edge of the trees and cabin beyond.

"Wildlife," Jake said thoughtfully, peering into the dense thicket where the traces of human passage faded into the randomness of animal life. "It makes you wonder if he knew how quickly his tracks would be lost among their patterns."

They spent another moment in silent contemplation, then moved on from the dead end of prints, retracing their steps back to the cabin and the slopes. And with every second that passed, Tessa started to feel unnerved by the way to prints simply disappeared. Though she knew it was silly, she couldn't help but feel as if they are chasing after a ghost.

CHAPTER THREE

Tessa and Jake navigated the narrow, fluorescent-lit corridors of the local forensics lab—a huge difference from the snowy grounds they'd left behind. It was a small, quiet area on the first floor of a brick building located directly behind the police station. It was a rather nice change from the sterile and somehow oppressive nature of the federal lab she was accustomed to. She followed Jake, her stride measured but her mind racing ahead.

They arrived at a room that was empty with the exception of two officers. The forensics lab was a small, crammed space, each surface littered with the detritus of ongoing investigations—papers, sample containers, and microscopes all jostling for room. One of the officers was in plain clothes, stationed at a laptop in the corner. The other was a rotund man who was currently hunched over a microscope. Tessa noted the precision in his movements, the scrupulous attention he paid to the object clutched in his latex-gloved hand.

As they drew closer, she saw that it was a snowflake pendant. The officer looked up as they approached, scrutinizing at first but slowly relaxing as both Tessa and Jake sowed their ID. He glanced at them through glasses that had slipped down the bridge of his nose, acknowledging them with a nod.

"Special Agents Flint and Sullivan," Tessa said. "Sheriff Bowen said we should come here looking for a Mr. Garcia."

"Look no further," the man said, giving a wave. "Pleased to meet you both. I assume you're here about the snowflake pendants, yes?"

"That's right," Tessa said. "Have you had the time to properly study them both?"

"I have."

"Any thoughts worth sharing?"

"Well, they are unmistakably the same necklace and pendant," Garcia said. With gloved hands, he carried the pendant he was currently observing over to a small table next to another microscope. The other pendant was there, the necklace laid out perfectly, as if on display. He set the other one directly beside it, and it was easy to see that he was right: the necklaces and the attached pendant were exactly the same.

“Are they made of real silver?” Jake asked.

“They are, though they really aren’t anything special. Not too expensive.”

“I assume you weren’t able to pull prints from them, were you?”

“Ah, well, I *did* pull a fingerprint from the first one but it turned out to belong to the victim, Elena Dean. I have to say, though, that I did just discover something of an abnormality on the one taken from Rachel Coolidge.”

“What kind of abnormality?” Tessa asked.

Garcia picked up the necklace he'd been studying and carried it back to his microscope. It was connected to a small laptop on the same desk, and when he pressed a button on the side of the microscope, what appeared on the lens also appeared on the screen. Tessa and Jake watched as Garcia placed the pendant back under the glaring microscope light. The pendant was then shown on the screen incredibly close up…so close that she could see the intricate details in the snowflake design.

Garcia used the tip of a pen to point out a specific area on the back of the pendant, revealing a minuscule puncture on the backside. "See this? This is not part of the original design. Too precise, too deliberate. You could miss it if you weren't really looking."

Tessa leaned in, her gaze sharpening as she examined the mark. She could just barely see the pin-prick hole, just large enough for a lance of some kind to poke through and pierce the skin. It was minuscule, yet its implications were vast, rippling through her thoughts. The possibility of it being used for something sinister sent a shiver down her spine, a sensation unfamiliar given her condition. Yet, she knew better than to jump to conclusions; their last case had been rife with injections and sedatives, and it was easy for the mind to draw parallels where there might be none.

Besides, out in the snow and the cold, there was no telling what sorts of nicks and cuts something like this could pick up.

"Could it be some kind of poisoning method, then?" Jake mused aloud, voicing the concern that hung unspoken between them.

"Too soon to say," Garcia replied carefully.

“Was there a similar puncture on the necklace taken off of Elena Dean?” Tessa asked.

“Not that I’ve found.”

Tessa stepped closer to the monitor, her eyes narrowed as she mulled over the profiles of themed killers, those who wove intricate tales through their choice of weapon or clue. If the pendant was indeed a symbolic piece of this chilling puzzle, then they needed to understand the narrative it was part of.

"Themed killers," she muttered, her tone contemplative as she turned away from the pendant to face Jake. "They often leave us breadcrumbs, don't they? Symbols that mean something to them, that tell their story."

"Right," Jake agreed, crossing his arms. "It's about the narrative they're crafting. More than just the kill—it's about sending a message."

"And what does our snowflake say?" Her eyes narrowed, focusing not on the object, but on the intangible idea it represented. "What is it telling us?"

"Uniqueness," Jake offered. "Every snowflake is different, like you said earlier. Maybe it's a signature?"

"Or an irony," Tessa countered. "Snowflakes are delicate, transient. But here, it's perverted into a tool for death. Psychological motives, maybe. If the pendant is a clue to the killer's mindset, then we're looking for someone who appreciates—or resents—the individuality of their victims."

"Like they're collecting one-of-a-kind trophies," Jake added darkly.

Tessa couldn't shake off the eerie sense of déjà vu, the shadow of their last case creeping into her consciousness. They had hunted a phantom who left a trail of bodies, each succumbing to a silent and unseen strike from a needle. She wondered if her mind was leaping to conclusions, the previous horrors bleeding into the fresh nightmare before them. Was she seeing patterns where there were none? Or was this truly the hallmark of a devious intellect at work?

Perhaps pushed by that eerie familiarity, Tessa asked: "Any luck tracing where it came from?"

"Not yet. But I do know that there are a pair of officers currently working to speak with every jeweler in town. If these pendants were bought locally, that could be huge. In fact…let me make a call and see how that's going. Give me just a few minutes, would you?"

Garcia switched deftly from his microscope to his phone, his thumbs swiping rapidly across the screen.

As Garcia dialed, his brow furrowing with concentration, Tessa leaned back against the cold metal table and pulled out her own phone. Her thumb hovered over the screen before diving into the digital files of the first victim, Elena Dean. Swiping through the autopsy reports and witness statements, she searched for something, anything that might spark a connection.

Elena Dean, a formidable force on the slopes, her stance aggressive, eyes fiery with unyielded ambition. It was a mirror image of Rachel—both women etched with the markings of victory, their lives defined by the razor-thin edge between triumph and defeat.

The competitive spirit that had propelled them to the apex of their sports was unmistakable. But now, Tessa pondered, could that same spirit have painted a target on their backs? Envy was a silent stalker in the world of elite competition, its whispers as dangerous as any physical threat. She considered the lengths to which one might go to sabotage a rival, to extinguish the brilliance they themselves could never claim.

As the shadows lengthened across the lab, the idea crystallized in Tessa's mind. Could the killer be among those whose dreams had crumbled, whose aspirations dissolved into the bitterness of what could have been? A failed athlete, a forgotten contender who watched as others soared to heights they could never reach?

As she scanned through the files, her eyes hung up on a name…a name that sounded slightly familiar: Kyle Brown. He'd worked as Elena's coach for three years, stopping just shy of a year ago.

And right around the same time, Elana had filed a restraining order against him.

"Why does that sound familiar?" she asked herself.

"What's familiar?" Jake asked.

"This name. Kyle Brown."

"I don't know. Is it a—"

But before Jake could offer an idea, Tessa thought she knew. She quickly switched over to Rachel's information, her phone now cascading with a series of open windows and files. She knew where to look because she'd poured over this very same information on the drive up here and…there it was.

His name was also in Rachel's file. Kyle Brown is also a coach for Rachel Coolidge.

Both women had been sculpted by the same hands, chiseled into champions under his tutelage. Sure, it could be a coincidence but in a case like this, *coincidence* was a dirty word as far as Tessa was concerned. Especially when the restraining order was considered.

The thought coiled in her gut, a serpent of suspicion. With each breath, the notion took root, spreading its tendrils through the dark soil of possibility. Kyle Brown had been their coach, their mentor. He's known their strengths, their weaknesses. His role offered him an intimate view into their lives, a front-row seat to the glory he could no longer grasp.

Determination hardened in Tessa's gaze as she locked her phone. She would start with Kyle Brown; he was the common thread linking the victims together. If there was darkness lurking behind his encouraging words and authoritative presence, she would unearth it. She would not rest until the truth was dragged into the light, even if it meant delving into the caverns of her own past.

"You got something?" Jake asked.

"Maybe," she said but it felt like more than a *maybe.* "Mr. Garcia, would you please mind letting us know if you find anything? We need to get going."

She reached into the inner pocket of her coat and produced a business card, which she handed him.

"Of course," Garcia said. "Is everything okay?"

"Not sure yet," she said as she headed out of the lab.

Jake followed quickly behind. "Do you want to tell me where we're headed?"

"I don't know yet," she said, pulling out her phone and scrolling to the number for the criminal database service in Portland. "It all depends on where Kyle Brown lives."

CHAPTER FOUR

The engine's low growl cut through the silence as Tessa navigated the sedan down a neglected, winding driveway. The driveway seemed to slither towards a house choked by overgrown vegetation. Jake sat beside her, his jaw set in a firm line, eyes scanning the environment with an intensity that matched her own. The former glory of the once-imposing house now lay buried under layers of decay and disrepair.

"Looks like Mr. Brown may have had quite the fall from grace," Jake said. "But if so, it was self-inflicted. The guy doesn't have a police report…not a single ding or red flag."

They'd discovered this during the drive, as Jake called for a background check while Tessa drove. Still, they'd both been in this field long enough to know that a blank slate wasn't an instant means of innocence. Kyle Brown was a strong link between both victims—strong enough for Tessa to hope that this case might very well be closed within the hour.

Tessa parked the car at the end of the driveway, the edges of which were slowly being overtaken by the thick, wild grass of the yard. As they stepped out of the car, the house loomed before them, its windows like hollow eyes and its paint peeling away like aged skin. It stood as a melancholy monument to a life that had dwindled into desolation. Tessa took a moment to let the scene etch into her memory—the perfect backdrop for a man living with secrets he had no intention of shedding.

"Cheery place," Jake remarked dryly, but Tessa only nodded, her attention snagged by the aura of decay. It was as if the house itself were a physical manifestation of Kyle's downfall, each broken shutter and sagging eave a metaphor for his shattered career. She could almost hear the whispers of failure clinging to the air, the silent echoes of dreams that had crumbled just like the mortar between the bricks.

They approached the door cautiously, Tessa leading with her well-practiced stride, ready for whatever might come. Oddly enough, neither of them got the chance to knock. The door opened as they stepped up onto the porch. It was so unexpected that Tessa noticed Jake's hand instinctually going for his Glock.

The man who greeted them was in his early forties. Ruggedly handsome, the lower half of his face was covered with a rather cliched beard—the sort of perfectly maintained, bushy beard trendy woodsmen sometimes sported.

"Yeah, who're you?" he asked.

"Are you Kyle Brown?" Jake asked.

"I am. And you? You're cops, right?"

With a skeptical glance to Brown, Tessa pulled out her badge and ID. "FBI, actually. And why do you ask? Seems like you've been expecting a visit from the cops."

"Not quite *expecting*. I guess you're here about Rachel Coolidge and Elena Dean?"

He asked it with such casualness that it made Tessa uncomfortable.

"We are," she said, keeping a cool and collected façade. "Would you mind if we came in and asked you some questions?"

"Yeah, that's fine. Just…well, the place is sort of a mess."

He waved them inside, and Tessa instantly saw that he wasn't just being modest. Not at all. Inside, the gloom of the house enveloped them. Sparse furnishings huddled in the corners of the living room shrouded in dust and shadows. The carpet bore the stains of neglect, and the walls were hung with pictures that had faded into ghosts of their former selves. The air was thick with the scent of the overflowing garbage bin in the kitchen and a faint cherry odor that she thought might be vape smoke.

"So, why mention Rachel and Elana?" Tessa asked.

"Well, I heard about Elana two days ago from her mother. I was always close with her family. But it was just this morning that I heard about Rachel."

"How'd you learn about it?" Jake asked.

"Facebook. One of her friends posted about her passing."

Brown sat down in a threadbare armchair. Though there was a couch sitting against the back wall of the living room, neither Tessa nor Jake sat down. Instead, Tessa took a single step closer to Brown and said, "Do you know why we're here?"

"I guess you want to ask me about them, right? I coached both of them and—if you don't mind me bragging a bit—I like to think I played a significant part in jump-starting their careers."

"But you quit coaching, right?" Jake asked.

"That's right. About three months after, Rachel moved on."

"And why did she move on?" Tessa asked.

She'd noticed that he was replying with words that stumbled over each other, hurried and clipped, as if trying to outrun the truth.

"You know, Rachel and Elana weren't the first girls I'd coached who went on to bigger and better things. I started to feel like a high school football coach, you know? You work to build, enhance, and train a player and then they go to college and it's all about recruiters and things. Now, Elana, she did keep in touch for a while but just sort of faded away. Rachel, though…as soon as she got the first big sponsorship and there was talk of the Olympics, she dropped me like a bad habit."

"Any particular reason?" Tessa asked, standing her ground as her instincts sharpened on the edge of his discomfort. She observed the small tells, the twitch of his fingers as they picked at the frayed fabric of the chair, the bob of his Adam's apple betraying a swallow too forceful to be casual.

And I haven't even asked him about Elana's restraining order yet, she thought.

"Everyone goes their separate ways," Brown answered, but there was a tremor in his voice that belied the nonchalance of his words. "I get it. And I tried very hard not to take it personally. But it got to me…and I quit."

"Separate ways that led them both to successful careers," Tessa countered, her gaze unwavering. "Careers you never had the chance to enjoy."

He bristled, the reaction immediate and telling. The room seemed to shrink with the tension that crackled between them, dense and foreboding as storm clouds.

"Success isn't everything," he spat, the veneer of calm shattering like thin ice underfoot.

"Maybe not to some," Tessa agreed softly, but her mind was already racing ahead, piecing together the puzzle of a man whose pride had been wounded, whose life was a testament to opportunities missed and bitterness harbored. She watched him closely, storing away each evasion, each defensive jerk of his limbs.

The story was unfolding, but she sensed that they were still missing vital pieces. And Kyle Brown was holding onto those pieces with a desperation that spoke volumes.

"There's another thing," Tessa said, ready to lay it all out. "I'd like for you to tell us why Elana placed a restraining order against you."

"Ah, God. *That* was blown out of proportion."

"Still…a restraining order can't just be ignored."

Kyle sighed, shaking his head. "For a few weeks, I was really worried Elana was going to turn her back on it all…on the sort she loved and had spent so much time working on. And there was this huge competition out in Colorado that I'd asked her to consider before we parted ways and she never decided. So on three occasions, I slid the flyer for it in her mailbox. One day, I even placed it under the windshield wiper of her car. She got *very* mad and filed that restraining order."

Apparently, the *you're-full-of-shit* expression on her face was evident because he chuckled and carried on.

"Yes, I know that sounds lame. But it's exactly what happened.

"Is there any proof of that?" Tessa asked.

"I'm not sure how to prove that. You could maybe ask her parents."

"Mr. Brown, when was the last time you spoke to either of them.Elana or Rachel?" Jake asked.

"I'm not sure. Well, with Rachel, it had been at least a year and a half, and that was just because we happened to run into each other at the slopes. But Elana…I don't know. Maybe three or four months. She called to tell me she was sorry for the restraining order…told me she'd ended up going out to that competition in Colorado and placed third."

"And what have *you* been up to ever since you quit?" Tessa asked.

"Not much, really. I…well, I had a job over in Sugarloaf. Just an instructor. But it didn't fit. When you've bene working for yourself for so long, it's hard to go back to the grind, you know?"

Tessa knew what she wanted to ask next. And she also knew that it may very well snap the already trembling sense of calm Kyle Brown was trying to uphold.

"Mr. Brown, where were you on the nights these women were killed?"

When he turned his gaze to her, she plainly saw the fury in his eyes. A vague sort of understanding filled them and he got to his feet as if he' been released from a spring.

"That's why you're here? You think *I* killed them?"

"You're our only solid link between them right now, so it makes sense to—"

But he had no intention of hearing Tessa out. He had been evasive, each answer a coil of smoke slipping through Tessa's probing questions. But now, there was a frenetic edge to him that put her on high alert. He began walking toward the door, and Tessa readied herself for what might come next. Was he going for a weapon, perhaps?

"Where do you think you're going, Mr. Brown?" Jake asked.

"Interview's over," Kyle grunted, his gaze fixed on the door. The room felt suddenly charged, the air thick with the scent of mildew and old sweat.

"Sit down, Mr. Brown," Tessa commanded. But Brown wasn't having any of it; he lunged for the door, his movements jagged with panic.

Tessa reacted instinctively, moving to block his path, her own body honed from years of training. When Brown reached out to move her, she saw the hesitation in the final breath of a second. He knew what he was doing was a mistake, that he was going over the line. But then his hand was on her forearm and that was all it took.

She caught Kyle by the wrist, her grip ironclad, but he twisted violently, a wildness overtaking his features. She sidestepped into the now-opened front door and pinned him against the doorframe.

She felt him trying to fight back for just a moment but then he seemed to understand that would be a mistake as well.

“Shit, okay,” he said. “I’m sorry. I wasn’t thinking. I shouldn’t have put my hands on you.”

Jake moved in then, the seasoned agent's presence both calming and reinforcing. He reached for his cuffs, but Tessa shook her head.

“I’m going to let you go, Mr. Brown. But if you run, I promise you that you’ll regret it. We just want to know where you were when Rachel and Elana were killed.”

“Yeah…okay. And like I said…I’m sorry. I just…I wasn’t thinking. I got mad at the accusation. Two of my past students gone in two days…I mean, it’s hard.”

Adrenaline speeding through her, Tessa stepped back and released him. Brown stepped back inside and stood in the center of the room with a look of shame on his face.

“Rachel was killed last night, right?” he asked.

“That’s right.”

“Last night, I was out at Blanky’s. It’s a bar in Langston. I spend too much time there, honestly. Closed the place down last night.”

“When did you get home?”

"Just before two in the morning. I had to wait on an Uber because I was in no shape to drive. It's why my car isn't outside. I've got a friend who's gonna give me a ride out there to pick it up later."

“I assume people at the bar can confirm this?” Jake asked.

“Yeah, at least five. And, like I said…my car will be there. I’ve also got the booking information for the Uber on my app.”

Without being asked to do so, he pulled his phone out of his pocket and pulled the information up. He showed it to Tessa and it was right there, plain to see: an Uber request for an address in Langston, filed at 1:14 in the morning. The fare was paid for at 1:48.

"Thank you, Mr. Brown. For your time *and* the information."

"Yeah, of course." He still looked embarrassed about how he acted, but the nerves were gone.

"Can you think of any enemies these women had?" Jake asked. His tone indicated he was irritated that Brown was clearly not the killer.

"Outside of competing athletes, no. I didn't really know them that well as of late."

Tessa knew the conversation and visit were over, so she wrapped it up. They'd come here for a killer but had instead found a man running from his past and struggling to start his life over. After another five minutes, they headed back outside, the evening air thick with the feeling of failure.

Jake was a silent shadow at her side; his footsteps in sync with hers, an unspoken pact between them. They'd gone in with cuffs and questions, armed with the authority of the badge and the sharpness of their minds. Yet they emerged handcuffed to uncertainty, the weight dragging at their spirits.

"Back to square one," Tessa muttered, her voice barely above a whisper. It wasn't just an admission of the moment but an echo of all the dead ends they'd faced before. The case was a labyrinth, and they were no closer to the minotaur at its heart.

"And where do you think that particular square might be?" Jake asked.

"The families," she said. "I think we pay visits to the families to see if they can offer more than Kyle Brown could."

They reached the car, its dark silhouette a stark contrast against the dying light. Tessa unlocked the doors, and as they settled inside, the interior wrapped around them like a confession booth. As they pulled away, Kyle Brown's house receded into the background, an unpleasant memory fading into insignificance. Ahead lay endless possibilities, each turn a potential revelation or another disappointment. But Tessa knew that the path of a good agent was not determined by the certainty of success—it is carved by the relentless pursuit of truth.

CHAPTER FIVE

The cold seeped through the fabric of Tessa's coat as she and Jake made their way up the porch stairs of the Dean home. It was a gorgeous house located in an upscale neighborhood, roughly forty minutes from the private slopes they'd started their case at. Even without stepping inside, Tessa got the feeling that this very nice home was currently more of a mausoleum, preserving the memory of a life cut tragically short. She stepped onto the front porch, her boots echoing on the wooden planks that led to the door.

"Ready?" Jake asked, his breath visible in the chill air, his tone deliberately even as if to balance the heaviness that hung between them.

Tessa knew what he meant. She dreaded speaking to grieving parents—perhaps because it reminded her far too much of how her father had reacted when Sarah had gone missing. It was the one weak spot to her agent toolbox, and Jake was always watching out for her in these situations.

"Yeah, I'm good."

As if to prove this, she reached out and pressed the doorbell with a determination that belied the uncertainty clawing at her insides. The sound seemed to travel through the house, a harbinger of the intrusion they were about to commit upon the family's sorrow. Time stretched until the door creaked open, revealing a tall man with shadows under his eyes that spoke of sleepless nights and a grief that refused to be consoled—very likely Elana's father.

"Yes?" he asked in a tired timbre.

"We're Agents Flint and Sullivan," she said. "We were hoping to speak with the parents of Elana Dean."

The man nodded and opened the door wider, ushering them inside. "Yes, please. I'm her father, Desmond. My wife is in the kitchen, putting on a pot for tea."

They stepped across the threshold, enveloped by the silence that only a home marred by loss could offer. It seemed the Deans had tried to maintain normalcy; pictures still smiled from the walls, the furniture sat undisturbed, but there was an emptiness in the air, a void that would never quite be filled again.

Tessa observed every detail with meticulous care—the way Mr. Dean's hands trembled slightly as he closed the door, the framed photograph of Elena on the living room mantlepiece, the bronze glint of a ski trophy catching the dim light. Each element was a potential clue, a possible insight into the life and death of their first victim.

"Did Elana live here with you and your wife?" Tessa asked.

"She moved out briefly for college but then when she realized she'd be traveling the country for tournaments and trials, she asked if she could just move in here rather than paying for an apartment or home she'd rarely be in." He frowned at the recollection of it all and then looked toward the hallway off of the living room. "One moment. Let me fill Doris in…let her know you're here. Would you like some tea?"

"Please. Whatever you're having," Tessa said. She had a habit of always accepting such offers from grieving parents. She wasn't sure why; it just seemed the proper thing to do.

She and Jake settled down onto a comfortable couch while Desmond went to get his wife. Tessa's gaze lingered on a particularly striking photo of Elena above the fireplace, poised at the top of a mountain, her expression a mix of concentration and excitement. Tessa could almost feel the chill of the alpine air, the adrenaline of the descent. But the warmth of the room and the soft ticking of a grandfather clock pulled her back to their grim reality.

Only a handful of seconds later, Mr. and Mrs. Dean entered the room. Doris Dean was carrying a small wooden tray with three cups of tea on it. A small sugar dish sat in the center. As she sat it down on the coffee table in front of the couch, Jake went through introductions again.

Tessa watched Mr. and Mrs. Dean cling to each other like two survivors in a life raft adrift at sea. The living room was a shrine to their daughter, the walls adorned with accolades of a life steeped in competition and victory. Her eyes traced over the Dean family, noting the hollowness in their gaze—the kind that spoke of sleepless nights and a pain that was more than just emotional.

"Can you tell us about Elena's last few months?" Tessa asked, her tone deliberately soft, not wanting to agitate the raw nerves exposed before her.

"She'd been practicing for an ice-skating camp," Mrs. Dean said. "She was working really hard to get into a show that travels the world. Sort of like a ballet on ice."

“I was going to ask about that,” Rachel said. “We knew she was an ice-skater but I see pictures of her skiing on the mantle there.”

“Oh, Elana was so good at *so* many things,” Mr. Dean said proudly. “She wasn’t at a pro-level with skiing, but she enjoyed it so much. But ice-skating was her one true love.”

“And where was she going to practice for this try-out?”

“Mostly Boston, but there were a few trips to New York as well,” Mrs. Dean said. “In fact, the final try-out is scheduled two weeks from now, in Manhattan.”

Tessa could tell she was fighting not to weep over this—a date her daughter had been very much looking forward to that she was not going to make.

"Can you think of t anyone who might have envied her success?” Jake asked. “Someone from the competitive circuit perhaps?"

Tessa watched for any flicker of recognition or discomfort. Both parents exchanged a glance, laden with unspoken words, before Mr. Dean answered. "I suppose, but that’s natural in any competitive sport. If she did have someone who was out for her, she never mentioned it to us.”

“Yes,” Mrs. Dean agreed. “And we never noticed anything... out of place."

"Any unusual incidents?” Tessa asked. “Any gifts or messages that seemed odd before..." Tessa trailed off, not wanting to finish the sentence.

"Nothing, that she told us about" Mrs. Dean said, closing her eyes as if to shut away the thought. "I do know that she had quite a fan following, though. Especially on social media. But again, if there was anything like that going on, Elana never said anything to us."

“You know,” Tessa said, “we just spoke with her old coach Kyle Brown. He seems to have fond memories of your daughter and said he was always close with your family. Would you have any reason to think he may have something to do with this?”

Mr. Dean shook his head at once. “No. I’d be shocked if that were the case. Kyle Brown has always been very respectable. A stand-up guy. And I hate that he is no longer coaching. I hear he’s sort of gone into a tailspin. But…well, that’s none of my business.”

“Elana spoke with him recently…at the slopes, I think,” Mrs. Dean said. “Though, I don’t know which ones. She said they got along well and loved getting to chat with him.”

Tessa figured this would be the case, but was glad she’d made sure.

The conversation waned, leaving Tessa with a haunting silence that settled heavily in the room. She noted each detail, understanding that sometimes what was unsaid could be as telling as the spoken word. Yet, her gut churned with frustration—this was not the breakthrough they needed.

Jake pushed along the remainder of the conversation, his questions gentle, probing the edges of the family's recollection for anything that might lead them to the second victim. Tessa listened, her mind sifting through responses, searching for the threads that might weave together to form a picture of their elusive killer. But as the minutes ticked by, it became increasingly clear that there were no clues here that would lead them to solid answers.

"I wonder," Tessa said after several minutes. "Mr. Dean, you said Elana had been living here. Would you mind if we had a look around her room?"

"Yes, that would be fine."

However, as he said this, Mrs. Dean's lips tightened and thinned. She nodded but got slowly to her feet. "Excuse me, please," she said.

When she was out of the room, having retreated back to the kitchen, Mr. Dean sighed. "She's having a very hard time accepting it. We all have, naturally… but it's absolutely wrecked her. She hasn't even stepped into Elana's room since it happened. But you're welcome to. It's up the stairs, the first hall on your right."

"Thank you."

They stood up together and followed the route Mr. Dean had given them. The found the stairs in the hallway and took them up. The door to Elena's room was closed and when Tessa opened it, she did so with great respect and reverence.

Tessa stepped across the threshold, her gaze immediately swept up in a sea of accolades that adorned every inch of the small sanctuary. Ribbons cascaded down like waterfalls of victory, their colors muted in the dim afternoon light filtering through the curtains. Trophies, gleaming even in the subdued glow, stood shoulder to shoulder on shelves that seemed to bow under the weight of triumph. And there, amidst the tangible echoes of success, were pictures of Elena—frozen smiles from atop snow-capped mountains, posing with other athletes, one candid picture of her looking off towards a slope.

Tessa moved further into the room, her fingers brushing against the cold metal of a trophy as she passed. The chill of it seeped into her skin, an unwelcome reminder of the life that had been snuffed out—a flame extinguished too soon. She paused before a photograph of Elena, caught in mid twirl in the midst of a beautiful skating formation, eyes alight with the fire of competition.

"Look at all this," Jake murmured, his voice barely above a whisper, lest it disturb the remnants of dreams scattered throughout the room. "She was more than just good. She was exceptional."

"Which makes it all the more tragic," Tessa replied.

As Tessa continued to survey the room, her analytical mind cataloged every detail—the layout, the personal touches, the potential for any clue that might lead them to the person responsible for extinguishing such a vibrant spirit. A letter, a gift, any token of appreciation or envy. Yet, as her eyes scoured the space and she looked through every drawer, there was a haunting absence of anything that pointed to why Elena had been targeted.

She reached out, fingers hovering over a medal that lay on a nightstand, not touching it but feeling its significance. Here was a young woman who had pushed herself to the limits, who had fought for every victory. The killer had taken more than a life; they'd stolen a legacy.

"Nothing," Jake finally said, echoing Tessa's thoughts. "There's nothing here that gives us a direct lead."

He was right. The room offered no answers, only the chilling reminder of a life ended too soon. And as they left Elena's room behind, the door clicked shut with a sense of finality that resonated deep within Tessa's core.

"Are you alright?" Jake asked, as he approached Tessa. His brow was furrowed with concern, an expression that made his eyes look quite intense.

"Yeah, just cataloguing," she replied tersely. Jake nodded, understanding that this was her process. Absorbing the environment, replaying conversations, searching for the anomaly in the pattern. He'd often teased her and said this was essentially her "downloading" the information.

"We need to see where Elana died," she suggested. "Maybe we'll get a better idea of next steps there. Or maybe the scene itself might reveal something."

"It's possible," Jake agreed.

Tessa nodded and slowly made her way out of the room. Her gaze lingered on one last trophy, thinking that maybe Elena Dean might have appreciated the fact that even after her death, people were still marveling at her accomplishments.

CHAPTER SIX

The dim glow of the dashboard illuminated his hands, skeletal in their stillness as they hovered over the steering wheel. Outside, the hockey rink buzzed with activity, a hive of parents and children, laughter and life – all oblivious to the darkness that watched from the car.

He sat motionless, a specter in the driver's seat, his gaze fixated through the glass barrier and onto the ice beyond. There, figures skated in joyous circles, but his eyes were drawn to one in particular. A young woman, Emily, gliding on the ice, her limbs moving with an ease that seemed as natural as breathing. She spun a pirouette of confidence and grace, her hair fanning out like the wings of an angel caught mid-flight.

His breath fogged up the windshield, his exhalations syncing with her rhythmic dance on the ice. He could almost feel the cool air against his face, the crisp bite of it stinging his lungs as he drew in a phantom breath of nostalgia. It was a painful yearning, a hunger for a past life. Once, he too had known what it was to own the rink, to command the silence before the storm of applause. But that had been another lifetime, a chapter closed and sealed within the pages of his twisted narrative.

Now, as he watched Emily's performance, it wasn't admiration that filled him, but a corrosive bitterness that gnawed at his insides. Her success was a mirror, reflecting his own inadequacies and failures. It was as though she skated atop the frozen fragments of his dreams, each leap and spin cracking the ice further, revealing the dark waters of his despair lurking beneath.

Her routine came to an end, and she rested against the wall that gave the rink its shape. Emily collected her breath while looking at something on her phone. She then put the phone away in a bag she had strapped a portion of the wall before heading back out on the ice.

As afternoon would toward evening over the rink, the killer's mind spiraled back in time. The pain surged first—a phantom ache in his knee, a haunting reminder of that fateful day on ice as cold and indifferent as fate itself. It was the day when a violent check against the boards warped the trajectory of his life, tearing ligaments and dreams in one cruel sweep. He had laid there, his breaths clouding above him, watching his aspirations bleed out onto the stark white rink.

As he remembered the grueling surgeries, the relentless physical therapy, and the ultimate betrayal of his body refusing to heal, a raw, guttural noise clawed up from his throat. The endless cycle of recovery and relapse played before his eyes like a grotesque film—his potential withering in the sterile light of the hospital room, his teammates moving on to victories and accolades while he became nothing more than a tale of caution, whispered in locker rooms and forgotten in record books.

He looked back out to Emily, a thin smile on her face—as if she might be smiling at his misfortune and suffering.. With each chuckle, she seemed to mock the future he could have had. The rink lights threw her shadow against the frosted glass, elongating her form into a specter of success—the very antithesis of what he had become. His hands clenched into fists, knuckles whitening as the vision blurred with unshed tears of rage.

He could almost taste the metallic tinge of resentment on his tongue as Emily landed another perfect jump. Effortless. Graceful. Everything he had once been and would never be again. A smoldering fury replaced the ache in his knee, spreading through his body with venomous warmth.

In the stillness of the car, where grief mingled with malice, his desire for vengeance fermented into something dark and potent. It was no longer about rectifying a personal wrong; it had evolved into a need to extinguish the brightness of those who reminded him of what was irrevocably lost. Emily had become the embodiment of every accolade that eluded him, every trophy he'd never hoisted, every cheer that wasn't for him. She didn't know it yet, but she had been marked by his scorn, a target for the pent-up rage of a glory that would never be reclaimed.

Still watching her, he reached into the depths of his coat pocket, fingers closing around a silver charm. It was a snowflake pendant, intricate and delicate. He'd already handed out two. And now, soon, Emily would get this one. The metal was chilling to the touch as he drew it out. For a fleeting moment, the icy burn of its edges against his skin was reminiscent of the biting sting of winter wind on a hopeful face years ago.

He held the pendant close, examining the minutiae of its design, each line and divot a haunting reminder of a past that was no more than a ghost now. This tiny piece of artistry, once a token of dreams and aspirations, had become a talisman of his bitterness, a symbol of what he once aspired to be and what he could never be again. He traced the snowflake's contours with a rough fingertip, contemplating how something so seemingly fragile had the power to weather the harshest storms—unlike his own broken ambitions.

His eyes lifted just enough to catch the flicker of movement at the rink's entrance. Emily was asking her exit, leaning against the outer wall and unlacing her skates. She was speaking to someone, chattering and laughing, unaware of the eyes that tracked her every step. As she moved beyond the halo of light cast by the rink and into the evening, he continue to watch, with the pendant still pressed between his fingers.

Silently, he acknowledged the inevitability of what was to come. Like the snowflake, which would inevitably melt away, leaving no trace of its existence, so too would Emily's light be extinguished. His preparations were meticulous, each detail as finely tuned as the routine she'd performed on the ice. The darkness of the car seemed to wrap around him, an accomplice to the sinister plan brewing in his mind. There was a perverse sense of patience within him, a predator's instinct to wait for the perfect moment to strike. But it wasn't time yet—not quite. Emily's departure was only the beginning of the end.

With deliberate motion, he slipped the snowflake token back into the confines of his pocket, its edges scraping against the fabric, whispering secrets of ice and despair. His hand lingered over the pocket, feeling the weight of the pendant against his thigh—an anchor tethering him to his purpose.

The silence within the vehicle was palpable, punctuated only by the faint ticking of the cooling engine and his own shallow breaths. The air seemed to grow heavier, charged with the imminent violence of his intent. He was no longer a man but a force of nature—a blizzard's heartless bite, an avalanche's unstoppable descent. The night outside the car stretched on, infinite and unknowing, waiting to be sliced apart by the cruelty that lurked within him.

With Emily out of sight, he turned the ignition; a throaty growl emanated from under the hood.. The car rolled forward, tires crunching over the frostbitten pavement, a steady rhythm that played counterpoint to the chaotic drumming of his blood.

As the vehicle gained momentum, the rink receded into the background, fading from view like a memory dissolving into the subconscious. He knew where he needed to go and what came next. He drove on in silence, a quiet that spoke volumes, a testament to the void that would soon claim another star that burned too brightly.

CHAPTER SEVEN

With each step toward the abandoned ice-skating rink, Tessa felt the weight of desolation pressing upon her; the hollow echo of laughter once shared within these walls now replaced by an oppressive silence. She walked to the edge of the frost-kissed floor of the old skating rink. Based on what they knew, the rink had closed down the day after Elana’s death—out of respect and a chance to install a new security system. Apparently, no one had done much in the way of maintenance since then because there were leaves and a few errant sticks that had blown in across the ice.

"We're looking for something we won't find," Jake muttered beside her, not sounding defeated exactly but forlorn and worried. The air was thick with dust motes that danced in shafts of light piercing through the holes in the canopy overhead. It seemed even the sun dared not shine too brightly here.

"Maybe," Tessa conceded, her eyes roving over the seating stands. “But patterns might emerge from where it all started." Her words were more for herself than for Jake. She needed to believe they were not walking in circles.

Tess walked carefully, mindful of the debris underfoot, her senses alert to every detail. Though the place had only been closed down a few days, there was something about the feel of the place that made it easy to imagine it old and abandoned. reeked of abandonment,

Here, in this decrepit rink, Elana Dean had taken her final breath. Tessa tried to picture the scene before the chaos to put herself in the shoes of the killer. What had driven them to this isolated spot? Why Elana?

"Look at this," Jake said, gesturing toward the far end of the rink. A small memorial, adorned with weathered flowers and cards, lay propped against the crumbling wall. A single teddy bear with a scarf and thick coat had fallen over onto its side. Tessa approached, her heart contracting. Amidst the tokens, a photo of Elana smiled back at her—forever young, forever gone.

"Elana was alone that night," she recalled, the details from the case file mingling with the grim reality before her. "Security footage showed no one else entered after her, but it also didn't show anyone leaving. Of course, there was just the one camera pointed at the parking lot."

“Good thing they’re adding more cameras during their downtime, then. Still…I mean, that suggests that our killer was already here, waiting," Jake finished the thought, the implications hanging heavy between them. "Or they found another way out, one the cameras didn't catch. And that’s very similar to how the killer managed to get away at Rachel Coolidge’s crime scene. He was already there, waiting, and managed to get away without leaving a trace."

"Either way, it doesn't leave us much to go on." Tessa's frustration was evident. They were standing at the epicenter of the mystery, yet it felt like they were miles away from the truth. She reached out and set the teddy bear back up.

"Let's take another sweep," she suggested, unwilling to succumb to the defeat that threatened to cloud her judgment. "We might have missed something, some piece of this sad puzzle."

Side by side, Tessa and Jake began their meticulous examination of the abandoned rink. But with each step, Tessa became more and more sure that the rink and its borders had nothing to offer.

They lingered there a moment longer, the silent tribute speaking volumes. But as they turned to leave, Tessa couldn’t shake the feeling of an unseen presence, as though the rink itself held its breath, withholding secrets just beyond their grasp.

"Where to next?" Jake asked, though it seemed more a formality than a question. They both knew the answer; it was etched in the grim set of his jaw and the determined glint in Tessa's eyes.

"Rachel Coolidge. We need to visit her parents.”

Jake nodded solemnly. “I’ll get their number and call ahead. It’s so recent…just twenty-four hours…hell, not even that. I figure the polite thing to do is call to make sure they’re up for visitors.”

Tessa nodded her agreement as they headed back to the car. The sky was bruised with twilight, the clouds hanging low as if mourning with them and knowing what came next. Another grieving family, another void to peer into. As they returned to the car, Rachel though the frigid air felt far too still, as if the world held its breath waiting for something sinister to unfold from the shadows.

***

The drive to the Coolidge residence was quiet. Jake drove while Tessa replayed the case in her mind, the lack of physical evidence, the obvious connection of winter sports between the victims. There had to be a pattern she was missing, a pattern that might reveal their killer.

The Coolidges lived in a two-story cabin five miles off of any main road. The little country avenues that led them to the house were winding and cast in an eerie yet beautiful glow as they drive through tangles of trees and overhanging branches at sunset.

The walk up to the front door felt longer than it should have, each step resonating with the dull ache of anticipatory grief. It was as though the air around the home was thicker, laden with the unseen weight of the Coolidges' mourning. Tessa's hand hovered over the doorbell, a small, inconspicuous button that served as the threshold between the outside world and the private realm of loss within.

Her finger pressed down, and the chime echoed, a sound too cheerful for the task at hand. The door opened slowly, revealing two hollow-eyed figures, the embodiment of sorrow etched deep into their faces. Rachel's parents stood at the door, a united front in their grief. The mother's eyes were red-rimmed, the father's handshake brittle with barely contained emotion.

"Hello. We're Agents Flint and Sullivan," Tessa said, her voice soft but firm. She could never truly understand their pain, but her empathy was genuine, a product of the depth of human suffering she'd seen in her line of work. "Thank you for seeing us."

"Anything to help find who did this to our girl," Mr. Coolidge replied, his voice breaking on the last word. He looked to be near sixty or so, and carried it well—one of those rugged-types who could probably pull of late-forties if he wore the right clothes. The Coolidges ushered Tessa and Jake into a living room frozen in time, Rachel's smiling face beaming from the photographs lining the mantelpiece.

It was a little too similar to the scene from the Dean house; in fact, it was downright eerie.

"We know you're dealing with an insurmountable loss," Tessa said, settling onto the edge of a floral-patterned couch that seemed out of place in the unfolding drama. "So we'll make it quick. There are a few typical questions we ask in these situations. We'll try those first and see if we can make this visit as quick as possible."

"Okay…" Mrs. Coolidge said. Her eyes were red and wandering as if she really wasn't even quite sure what was going on.

"I know it may seem like an odd question," Jake said, "but could you tell us if Rachel had any enemies? Anyone who might've wanted to harm her?"

The question didn't seem to surprise them, perhaps because they'd likely been wondering the same thing ever since learning of their daughter's murder.

"I really can't think of a single person who disliked her," Mrs. Coolidge answered, wringing her hands, the fabric of her skirt twisting between her fingers. "Of course, there may have been some folks in her personal life that she just never told us about, but…for right now, no…I can't think of a single person."

"Now, I don't know if this would count," Mr. Coolidge interjected after a heavy pause, "but her ex-boyfriend wasn't taking the breakup well. He was quite insistent they get back together."

"What's his name?"

"Joseph. Joseph Redding."

"Insistent how?" Jake asked, leaning forward, his detective's interest piqued.

"Showing up to her apartment uninvited, sending messages. Things like that."

"That's right," Mrs. Coolidge said, as if she'd completely forgotten. "She had blocked him on her phone and he even came by here looking for her a few times."

"Was he ever aggressive?" Tessa inquired.

"Verbally, yes. Always wanting another chance." Mr. Coolidge's voice held a quiver of anger now, a father's protective fury simmering beneath the surface. "But we never thought..."

"I don't think Joseph would ever raise a hand to her, if that's wat you're getting at," Mrs. Coolidge said. "They were together for almost two years and we got to know him fairly well."

"Still," Mr. Coolidge said. "He *would* get pretty angry whenever she blocked him out."

"Do you know why they broke up?"

"Because snowboarding came first and Joseph couldn't accept that. Also, about three months ago, he cheated on her from what I understand. It was a week when she was out at a competition…somewhere out in Wyoming."

"When was the last time you saw him?"

The Coolidges shared a look that ended when Mr. Coolidge shrugged. "Maybe two weeks ago?"

"And do you know, by any chance, if Rachel happened to know another athlete by the name of Elena Dean?"

Mrs. Coolidge's eyes showed recognition but she thought about it for a moment. "I'm sure I'd heard Rachel mention that nae before, but it would have been in passing I'm quite sure they weren't friends or anything. She's a…an ice skater, right?"

"Right."

"I think they may have participated in a charity event together last year, but that was about it. And even that…you know, I'm not positive."

Tessa waited a moment, processing it all before she went on. "Do you recall anything that seemed out of the ordinary over the past month or so?" she asked.

"You know," Mrs. Coolidge said, turning her attention to Jake, "we were talking about that not long before we got your call, Agent Sullivan. And there *was* one thing that seemed odd and maybe even threw Rachel off a bit. It didn't seem like a huge deal, but…"

"What was it?" Tessa asked.

"Someone sent Rachel a necklace through the mail. A snowflake pendant. There was no return address, so we don't know who sent it. We figured it was maybe Joseph."

"How long ago was this?" Tessa asked, her heart pounding a bit heavier at this intense news…this possible connection. She exchanged a look with Jake. An anonymous gift, a pushy ex—these were the first solid leads they had. It was something to pursue, a glimmer of hope in the darkness.

"The necklace? About two weeks ago."

"Did you ever see it?" Jake asked.

"Yes. She took a picture of it and sent it to me," Mrs. Coolidge said. She grabbed her phone from the coffee table and pulled the picture up.

When Tessa saw the photo, her heartbeat sped up even more. It was the exact same pendant that she'd been wearing.

"Do you know if she wore it often?" Tessa asked.

"She didn't. She was sort of creeped out by it, I think. Someone just sending her an anonymous gift. She's had young girls write her letters and asking her questions about ow to get started with a career in snowboarding and things like that. But never an anonymous gift."

This is it, Tessa thought. *This is where we hit a solid track and forge on until the case is closed.*

"Is it…do you think this necklace has something to do with the murder?" Mr. Coolidge asked.

Tessa knew the truth might make their grieving harder—a truth that told them another winter athlete had been murdered while wearing the exact same pendant.

“We can’t know for sure,” she lied. “But all of this has been an enormous help. Thank you so much for your time.”

With a quiet gratitude and a promise to do all they could, Tessa and Jake rose, the clues. The clues they had gleaned pushed them on with new encouragement. Outside, twilight was leaning closer to night, the day’s last dying light falling over the yard. Their shadows stretched long over the grass.

"Joseph is our next move," Tessa stated, her voice betraying none of the frustration that had nagged at her since they began the case.

Jake nodded, his expression grave as they walked to the car. He was already on his phone pulling up the resource number to have someone get them the address for Joseph Redding.

Rachel knew an ex-boyfriend could be a wildcard—a potential aggressor cloaked in the vestiges of romantic attachment. She’d seen it more than once as an agent. Unrequited love and a broken heart could often drive men to do bad things—to line them up with a darkness inside of them they’d never known existed.

They drove in on with a mutual understanding between them that words were unnecessary. In their silence, they were each lost in thought, piecing together the puzzle that seemed to grow more complex with each revelation. And at the end of it all, hopefully enough answers to capture a killer.

CHAPTER EIGHT

Night had begun to properly fall as Tessa pulled into the lot in front of Joseph's apartment building. The apartment building was in the quiet, mostly forgotten little town of Averson, roughly fifteen miles away from the Coolidge residence. It was a drab, brick structure, with peeling paint on the window frames and a weathered wooden staircase leading up to the second floor where Joseph's unit was nestled at the end.

They climbed the creaking stairs, the sound unsettling in the still air. Tessa's hand hovered over her gun holster, more out of habit than necessity. She knocked sharply on Joseph's door, the metallic rap echoing slightly. There was a shuffling from inside, the muffled sound of feet padding across a hard floor, and then the door swung open abruptly. Joseph Redding stood there, his face betraying both surprise and annoyance, the lines around his eyes crinkling in suspicion.

“Yeah?” he said, clearly confused over the arrival of his visitors. “Can I help you?”

"Special Agents Flint and Sullivan," Tessa said in way of greeting, showing her badge with an almost magician-like flick of the wrist. "We were hoping to ask you some questions regarding Rachel Coolidge."

Joseph crossed his arms defensively, the muscles in his jaw twitching ever so slightly. "What about her?" he asked, his voice guarded. “Are you trying to find the heartless bastard who killed her?”

“You could say that. May we come in?”

It was clear just by his expression that having FBI agents in his apartment might be the last thing he wanted, but he agreed anyway. There was a slight sneer on his face as he invited them inside.

Inside, the apartment felt claustrophobic, cluttered with books and unopened mail. It wasn’t a dump by any means but it did hold a few signs that man lived alone here; it wasn’t anything specific, just a vibe from the way the place was set up and decorated. Nothing *really* matched up in terms of furniture or the pictures and art print son the wall. As she took it all in, she noticed a picture of Rachel Coolidge moments after hitting a jump, her body and board suspended in the air.

Without a word, Joseph led them through a small kitchen into the living room. Tessa sat down on a frayed couch, noting how Joseph took a chair across from them, creating a physical barrier with a coffee table.

"So how do you think I can help?" Joseph asked. "I guess you already know she dumped me and we'd been apart for a few months."

Tessa took note of how irritated he sound as he spoke. If he was their killer, he had decided not to attempt playing the role of the devastated ex. Instead, he sounded angry. The question, of course, was *why?*

"Yes, we're aware of that," Jake said.

"Tell us about your relationship with Rachel," Tessa prompted.

She watched Joseph closely, her gaze sharp and unwavering. She was trained to spot the smallest discrepancies, to hear the lies hidden in the tremor of a voice or the too-quick denial. "Well, when it was good, it was *really* good. Sort of a whirlwind romance. If we ever fight, it was over stupid shit like movies and music. I miss her. I missed her even before…well, before *this."*

"Apparently, you missed her enough to get a little aggressive about trying to get her back."

Joseph nodded, his eyes going to the coffee table in what looked like shame. Tessa She dissected his every gesture—the way he avoided eye contact when talking about the breakup, the clench of his fists when he mentioned how he missed her.

"That's fair," he said. "I take it you've spoken to her parents?"

"We did. Listen, Joseph…we need to know where you were last night. Given what we know about your approach over the past few weeks in trying to get her back, we have to at least consider that you—"

"Yeah, I figured. I get it, I guess. But I can tell you right now, I was nowhere near her last night. The last time I tried convincing her to get back together with me…it was the last straw, you know? A guy can only take so much rejection."

"But you clearly still care for her," Tessa said, pointing to the frame picture of Rachel on the wall, forever frozen in the midst of an epic jump.

He nodded, and when he looked up at her, she could see the hurt in his eyes. He *was* feeling the loss but doing his best not to let it get to him. She hated to assume someone's innocence so soon, but she saw all she needed to see right there. Still…she had a job to do.

"So…where were you last night?"

"I'm not particularly proud of it, but I was sitting here…in this apartment, on my ass, playing video games."

"Was anyone with you?" Jake asked.

"No. But all of the gameplay was online. Fortnite for a bit, and then a lot of Madden."

"Are there logs for that sort of thing?" Tessa asked.

"Madden catalogs the games played…wins and losses," Josephs said. "And with Fortnite…I don't think there's anything like that. But I can give you the usernames of the people I was playing with."

"And we can use your username and contact the servers for confirmation," Jake said.

"How long were you on?"

"I'm not sure, exactly. I do know I stayed up way too late. I wrapped my last game of Madden around two in the morning." He shrugged and added: "When you're single around here, there's not much to do. And I am, as you know, very much single now…so…"

"During the time you were trying to get her back, did you ever send her any gifts through the mail?" Tessa asked.

"Flowers—a bouquet of roses. That was about six weeks ago."

"And that's it?"

"Yeah, that's all."

Tessa hated that she already had an opinion formed, but she soldiered on anyway. "We heard from the Coolidges how you two ended up breaking up. Do you want to tell your side?"

He scoffed, but not in a dismissive way. It seemed that the more he was being forced to talk about this, the more he was realizing just how badly he was hurt.

"I can, but it's pretty simple. I fell in love *hard* at the start of our relationship. And after about….maybe nine months or so, it became very clear that there was no way I was going to win out over snowboarding. I mean, it was basically her religion. And if I made a single negative comment about her always being on the road or overseas or at another frigging practice she didn't need, she made it very clear what her priorities were. And there was a point where I think I just griped about it too much, and she was done. And you've spoken to her parents, so you know I didn't exactly handle it well."

Tessa nodded and stood up from the couch. "Mr. Redding, we may end up running you online information just to prove your alibi. Would you be cooperative with us if we went that route?"

"Absolutely. I…I don't know how I feel about this loss right now, but…I know it hurts. I know I miss her and whoever did this to er needs to pay. So, yes…you let me know what you need, and I'll help."

"Thank you. And have a good night."

Slowly, Tessa and Jake made their exit. Tessa took note of how Jake took one last lingering glance around the apartment on their way out. For a handful of seconds following their departure, things were quiet between them as they made their way back down the stairs to the first floor.

"Here's the thing," Jake said, finally breaking the silence, his voice tinged with frustration. "I believe him. I don't think he killed her, but until we can get verification that he was playing games online that entire time, we can't know for sure. And I can't shake this feeling... like we're missing something critical."

Tessa nodded in agreement. Joseph's behavior had at times felt too practiced, too controlled. It was the performance of a man who had rehearsed his innocence, but to what end?

"I'll put a call in to Sheriff Bowen and ask them to keep tabs on him for a while." She thought it was a justified measure. She didn't fully trust that Joseph was innocent, but she couldn't ignore the evidence—or lack thereof—that pointed elsewhere.

Tessa felt the weight of expectation pressing down on her. As agents, they were trained to follow the evidence, yet her intuition whispered of darker currents beneath the surface. She had learned to trust that voice over the years, and it had never led her astray. With renewed determination, she resolved to uncover the truth, no matter how deeply it was buried.

"So here's the next big decision," Jake said. "Are we staying around here overnight or heading back to Portland?"

"I say stay here," she answered without much thought. "I know it's only about two hours, but I feel like this thing could break at any moment. I'd rather be here, in the center of it all."

"Agreed."

They walked into the night, to their car. And as they drove away, Tessa peered through the rearview mirror at Joseph's apartment fading into the distance. The pendants, those delicate symbols of winter's beauty turned macabre tokens of death, loomed large in her thoughts. They were a message, a signature…but from whom?

CHAPTER NINE

There were no chain hotels in the area—the closest one was over half an hour away—so they settled for the only one close to the private slopes where Rachel had been killed, and the skating rink where Elana had met her end. It looked very unappealing from the outside against the bitter cold, but the interior actually wasn't bad at all.

The room was standard fare: a bed with a quilted coverlet, a small desk with a lamp, and curtains that blocked out the rest of the world. Dropping her bag on the chair, Tessa exhaled slowly, trying to quiet the echoes of the investigation that persisted in her mind. Tessa wasted no time in sitting up a little workstation on the square, featureless table by the bed—not the bedside table, but the sad little two-person table that often sat sad and forgotten in the corner. As her laptop powered up, she looked out of the window to the glimmering streetlight in the parking lot. With a deep breath that did little to ease the weight on her chest, she peeled back the curtains and returned to her solitude.

She dove into the case files, using her laptop and phone to juggle through with greater speed. Witness statements seemed to blur into one another, victims' lives reduced to bullet points and sterile facts. Absently, her finger traced the touchpad, navigating through the maze of information as her mind worked tirelessly to piece together what eluded her grasp.

Her eyes, weary yet unyielding, scanned the case files that illuminated her laptop screen in the dimly lit room. Each word, each comma, every slight nuance within the witness statements was devoured by her relentless gaze. She dissected professional backgrounds of victims like a surgeon, tracing their lives for patterns or anomalies. The descriptions of crime scenes unfolded before her, a grim tapestry of details that she hoped would eventually reveal the murderer hiding within its threads.

The victims shared the very obvious connection of winter sports—women who were all very good in their chosen sport. Tessa sifted through their accolades and achievements, searching for a connection that might have drawn the killer's ire. A photograph of Rachel Coolidge, smiling at an awards ceremony with her board tucked under her arm, seemed to mock Tessa's efforts from the cold glow of the screen.

Shifting in her seat, Tessa opened a new file, one filled with pictures of the snowflake pendants—each one left at a crime scene, a signature of sorts from the killer. They were delicate, intricate, and hauntingly beautiful in their design. It was a cruel contrast to the violence they represented. Tessa zoomed in on the high-resolution images, studying each line and curve of the silver filigree. There was a meaning there, hidden within their frosty symmetry, and she felt it just out of reach—like a word forgotten on the tip of the tongue. She made a note to reach out to the police or forensics department again, wondering if there had ever been any news on where the pendants may have been purchased. It would be convenient if they'd come from a local jeweler, but Tessa was all but certain they would have been ordered online—that is, if the killer knew what they were doing. And if that was the case, finding the source would be next to impossible.

"Unique, but not custom-made," she murmured to herself, reading a note from forensics out loud.

Her mind raced with theories—symbols of perfection, of uniqueness, a representation of the transient nature of life, perhaps? Or was it an allusion to the coldness of their own soul? She ran her hand through her hair, frustration mounting. She wanted, needed to understand the perverse poetry behind the pendants. But the pieces refused to fall into place, slipping through her mental grasp like shadows at dusk.

As night wrapped tighter around her and she found herself afloat on the digital glow of case files that presented only further questions, Tessa couldn't help but let her thoughts drift toward Sarah. The cold case that never thawed, a constant chill in Tessa's bones. Despite the years, despite the distance, it always found a way to seep through the cracks in her armor. She swiped away photographs of crime scenes, replacing them with the yellowed images of her sister, the fading flyers that once signaled hope now nothing more than digital ghosts.

Opening the private folder marked 'Sarah,' Tessa dove into the abyss of old clues and theories. Each document was a testament to desperation, each interview a reminder of dead ends. Still, she combed through them, searching for anything that might spark a new perspective, any thread that could weave together the past and present. She could recite each line by heart, but she knew that meant nothing. It often made her think of preachers who read the same fragments of scripture over and over, committing the words to heart yet somehow always finding new meaning. That was what she was hoping for. That's what she'd *been* hoping for over the last six or seven years.

Sarah, with her laugh that seemed to light up the room, her fiery spirit so different from Tessa's own quiet resilience. It was a difference born both of personality and necessity; Tessa's inability to feel physical pain had rendered her life one of constant vigilance, a paradoxical existence where injury went unnoticed unless seen. But it had also been that very same condition that had fascinated Sarah. There were times where, in a sisterly and rather goofy way, they'd toy with poking Tessa with sewing needles—nothing morbid, just pin pricks. It had always astonished Sarah…the idea that her sister couldn't feel pain.

"Like a superhero," Sarah had said more than a few times.

"Yeah, a superhero who can't find you," Tessa whispered into the hotel room.

She could still recall the day of Sarah's disappearance with crystal clarity—the chaos, the fear, the police swarming their home, asking questions to which no one had answers. The slow and sad unraveling of her father, a policeman who'd been useless in the search to find his daughter. It had been years, but the mystery remained, gnawing at Tessa, demanding attention. Tessa let out a sigh that felt as if it came from the depths of her soul and opened a private folder on her laptop—a collection of documents, photos, and notes about Sarah's case.

The files held the remnants of countless hours spent searching for something everyone else had missed. There were scanned copies of police reports, maps marked with possible sighting locations, interviews with friends and acquaintances, anything that might lead to some semblance of truth. Each file was meticulously named and organized, a testament to Tessa's relentless pursuit of closure.

Tessa scrolled through the list of files until she found what she was looking for—an old theory she'd developed after noticing a pattern in the few leads they had. She clicked it open, the document filling her screen with conjecture about a car spotted near their neighborhood around the time Sarah vanished, a car with out of state plates.

Tessa leaned back in her chair, feeling the weight of years sitting heavy on her shoulders. In the sterile light of her laptop, surrounded by the ghosts of unsolved mysteries, she allowed herself to dwell in the possibility that solving the present case might somehow bring her a step closer to understanding what happened to her sister. It was a spark she felt at least once in every case she took on. She knew it was a naïve hope, but she also knew it was a hope that kept her going—that made her a bit sharper and more dedicated than most other agents.

In the glow of the laptop screen, her father's face, worn and weathered from years on the force, flashed in her mind's eye—a beacon of wisdom, yet a reminder of how often she fell back on him when darkness clouded her judgment. Tonight, however, she couldn't afford to let sentimentality be her guide. She needed to stand on her own, to prove not just to her father, but to herself, that she could unravel this twisted tapestry without his threads of insight.

Tessa reached for her phone, her fingertips grazing the cool metal surface before she withdrew her hand as if scorched by the very idea of dependence. No, she would not call him. Her resolve was a dam holding back the floodwaters of doubt.

She considered Elle, her mentor and a steady fixture during her time at the academy. Elle's analytical mind had steered Tessa through many a case, her mentorship a compass in the wilderness of crime solving. The thought of hearing Elle's steady voice, grounding her in logic, was almost too tempting. As Tessa hovered over the contact in her phone, a sharp trill sliced through the room's silence. Her phone vibrated and rang in her hand, giving her a small fright.

Embarrassed and slightly sad from the whirlwind of memories, she answered as quickly as she could.

"This is Agent Flint," she answered, her voice steadier than she felt.

"Tessa, it's Sheriff Bowen." The urgency in his tone snagged her full attention. "We've got another one—another victim with that damned pendant around her neck."

"A winter athlete?"

"We think so. It's all very fresh, so we're checking on that right now...but it seems like it."

"What's the location?"

As the sheriff relayed the scarce details over the line, a surge of adrenaline coursed through Tessa, washing away the remnants of her personal turmoil. Sarah's shadow receded into the corners of her mind as the professional façade clicked into place, a mask of composure over a maelstrom of emotions.

"We'll be there as quickly as we can," she said curtly, disconnecting the call with a decisive press. She instantly brought up Jake's number as she closed her laptop cover and slipped back into her shoes.

Outside, the night was thick and dark, but it seemed like their day was far from over.

CHAPTER TEN

The last stretch of road that took Tessa and Jake to the new crime scene was little more than a dirt road that wound back into the hill-choked forest. It was just after 11:00 when Jake turned the car off of the basic two-lane and onto the unmarked stretch of road lined with gravel. Tessa noted a few houses tucked into the trees along the road but the entire length of it seemed isolated—almost like something out of a horror movie.

Near the end of the road, just past a sign that read END OF STATE MAINTENANCE, there was a small turn-off to the right. Though the entire road was shrouded in the night and overhanging trees, the turn-off was impossible to miss. The glow of headlights and the bobbing of several flashlight beams could be seen even before Jake took the turn.

This new road was only about fifty yards long. It came to an end in a slanted, square-shaped turnaround spot. There were three police cruisers on the scene; four different men were walking along a field to the left, flashlights aimed at the ground. Ahead of them, supped between grass that was just barely snow-covered and the surrounding forest, was a small pond.

The skeletal trees clawed at the grey sky, their bare branches like bony fingers beckoning secrets from within the woods. The pond itself was frozen over, but even a simple glance at it told Tessa that the ice wasn't thick enough to support anyone. All the same, there was a jagged section of broken ice on the side of the pond closest to the trees.

According to what Bowen had told Tessa on the phone, the third victim had been discovered in that spot. She could see where the body had been pulled out, a lump on the bank, covered up by a blanket. As she and Jake walked over to the pond and the gathered cops, Tessa's breath materialized before her in short puffs, the cold air nipping at her lungs.

Sheriff Bowen stepped out of the cluster of cops to approach them. "Thanks for coming so quickly."

"Of course," Tessa asked. "Do you mind if we run with it for a few minutes?"

"Consider the scene all yours."

“Who pulled the body out?” Tessa asked.

“That was me. And I’m the only one to touch her. Used a fallen branch from the woods to pull her closer to the bank and then I grabbed her under the armpits to pull her out.”

What’s the victim’s name?”

“Emily Radley. And we *have* just confirmed that she’s a professional skater. She grew up around here but lives in Rhode Island. She was in town to see her folks.”

“What else do we know about her?”

As she asked questions, they avoided the cluster of cops as they made calls to the coroner and forensics. Bowen followed behind them, allowing for a respectable distance. They walked around the edge of the pond—an almost perfect circle of water that Tessa estimated might be about sixty or seventy feet wide and short enough to throw a rock across of the throw really got some heft behind it.

“She’s twenty-three, dating a local guy. According to the boyfriend, he found her like this. He said they’d made plans to sort of sneak out here and fool around…trying to recapture the fun and excitement they had when they were teens.”

“On the way to the station. He flipped out…an emotional wreck. He was actually throwing up because he was weeping so hard.”

“Any suspicions it was him?”

“No, he’s innocent. He was coming from work to meet her and we already confirmed that with his supervisor.”

They’d come to the edge of the pond where Emily Radley’s shape was covered in a nearly loving way by a blanket; Tessa assumed Bowen had placed it there. Tessa approached the broken ice with methodical steps, noting how the serene stillness of the pond contrasted sharply with the violence of the crime. Sheriff Bowen stood by quietly, his face etched with concern under his furrowed brow. She could sense Jake's presence behind her, steady and watchful. Her eyes swept over the scene, cataloging every detail: the way the ice had splintered outward from the point of impact, the muffled sound of their footsteps on the snow, the footprints creating a mess around the bank of the pond and then escaping out into the forest.

It was an eerie tableau, nature's beauty turned sinister by the presence of death. Each step took her deeper into the heart of the crime scene, the periphery of her vision catching the minutiae that others might miss—the uneven pattern of footprints, the slight disturbance of the snow that blanketed the ground, the remnants of a struggle etched into the winter canvas.

"Looks like she went through here," Tessa murmured, pointing to the fractured ice. Sheriff Bowen nodded solemnly, gesturing to the body that lay on the bank, a blanket draped over it like a macabre shroud. As Tessa moved closer to examine it, the pang of urgency for justice for these victims fueled her focus. She knelt down beside the figure, carefully lifting the blanket. The victim wore a winter jacket much like the first two, and around her neck was that damned snowflake pendant, glinting with a mocking sparkle amid the tragedy.

"If she was an experienced skater, she'd know this ice was too thin to go out on," Jake said.

"I was thinking the same thing," Bowen said.

"I don't think it was a wrong decision on her part," Tessa said. "I think someone threw her in."

"Those prints?" Jake asked.

"Yeah."

All three of them turned around and observed the mess of footprints. It was the same method and approach they'd seen at the private slopes where Rachel Coolidge had been killed. Someone was purposefully trying to throw them off, knowing the footprints could be followed.

"Is this a popular spot for locals?" Tessa asked.

"Kids usually play here when it's frozen solid," Sheriff Bowen. "Hockey and amateur skaters. Emily's boyfriend said Emily sometimes practiced out here when she was in high school. And later, when they got more serious, he said they came out here to...well, like I said. To do the things teenage couples do."

Tessa continued to take in the scene as Jake took his phone out of his coat pocket and began snapping pictures.

"You think she was already dead when the body was thrown in?" Bowen asked.

Rachel turned to Emily's body and began to look at her neck, trying to determine an answer to Bowen's question. But as she did, before she was able to get a good look and make a determination, she caught a movement out of the corner of her eye. It was so minor that she thought it was just the strange play of dark tree shapes against the snow on the ground. But as she turned her head and focused, squinting into the dense trees, she discerned a lone figure standing motionless, almost blending with the barren trunks.

"Someone's out there," she said in a calm tone, just loud enough to notify Jake and Bowen. "Don't react harshly. Just follow my lead."

She got to her feet again, slowly turning back in the direction of the forest where she'd seen the figure. Even before she saw the figure again, she said, "I know you're out there. Do us a favor and come down here. We need to talk to you."

Behind her, Bowen had apparently spotted the figure, too. He muttered a curse under his breath. Slowly, Jake stepped up beside her.

"See them? Tessa asked.

"Yeah."

Tessa's eyes had found the figure again, too. It appeared to be a man, though from this distance—about thirty or forty feet—it was hard to tell. They were dressed in thick clothes and wearing a ski cap. They were standing directly beside a tree, their right hand placed on it as if they planned to move it in front of them as a shield if it came down to it.

And then, with all three sets of eyes on them, the figure apparently decided it was just too much.

They ran.

"Hey!" Tessa called out, her voice authoritative and loud enough to startle a nearby crow into flight.

Instead of complying, the figure bolted deeper into the forest. A shot of adrenaline surged through Tessa's veins, and without a second thought, she took off after the fleeing shadow.

"Jake!" she shouted over her shoulder, already in pursuit.

"Right behind you!" Jake's response came from behind her, his footsteps pounding the ground in tandem with hers as they sped off into the night-shrouded forest.

CHAPTER ELEVEN

They raced through the snowy underbrush, dodging low-hanging branches and leaping over gnarled roots. Tessa's heart hammered in her chest, the icy air sharp in her lungs. Her disability meant she could push harder, ignore the pain signals that might have slowed others down—from high impact on ankles, knees and lungs. But it also meant she had to be vigilant against injury without the warning system of discomfort.

The figure ahead moved with desperate speed, darting between trunks, their breaths visible in the cold air. Tessa focused, her keen eyes taking in every detail—the height, build, the way they moved—with an intensity that burned.

"Stop! FBI!" Jake's command boomed through the trees, but the figure only pushed harder, their form becoming more elusive as the light dimmed beneath the thickening canopy overhead.

Tessa's thoughts narrowed to the chase, the relentless drive to capture what could be a vital piece in the puzzle. Branches whipped at her face, leaving thin lines of red against her skin, unnoticed in her fervor. She could almost reach out and grab the suspect, could almost feel the triumph of closing her fingers around their arm.

"Watch out!"

Jake's warning cut through her focus, and she narrowly avoided a ditch, concealed by snow and deadfall. She looked down just in time, and her agility saved her from a nasty fall.

The figure moved with a panic-laced precision, the movements of someone who knew these woods well. With a final burst of energy, Tessa followed behind, determined to end the pursuit and uncover the truth lurking within the shadowed woods.

The air was sharp as a blade, each breath Tessa took cut through her lungs like she was inhaling icicles. Her boots were sinking into the snow, half a foot deep in places, which clung to her legs and tried to pull her down with every step. Darkness enveloped the woods, the kind of darkness that felt alive, reaching out with shadowy fingers to snag on her clothes and slow her escape. The trees were skeletal silhouettes against the night sky, branches clawing at the stars.

She focused on the trail left by the suspect, the disrupted whiteness of the ground beneath the trees. Suddenly, she realized the footprints were fresher, the edges of the indents in the snow sharper. He was close. Her heart pounded in her chest, a drumbeat urging her forward, as she pushed through a thicket of underbrush and saw the figure not twenty feet ahead.

If she had to, she'd pull her Glock and fire a warning shot. But that was only as a last resort.

"Stop! FBI!" she called out, but the figure only glanced back with a sneer before running faster.

Then came a muffled curse from behind her. Tessa turned her head just in time to see Jake stumble and fall into a deeper drift, his body disappearing into the white for a moment before he struggled to right himself. His face was etched with frustration and the cold.

"Go!" he gritted out, waving her forward with a determined glare. Tessa hesitated for only a fraction of a second before turning back to the chase, knowing Jake would catch up. They were a team, but right now, the immediate task at hand was hers alone to tackle. She pushed harder, her legs burning, her breath a ragged symphony in sync with the pounding of her heart.

More branches slapped her in the face and snatched at her FBI jacket, but she was relentless. This was what she lived for—the hunt, the challenge, the resolve to capture those who believed they were beyond justice. She was almost upon him, her hand reaching out to grab his arm, when he abruptly turned to confront her.

"Stop!" she shouted, her voice cutting through the night, commanding and clear. But the figure pushed forward, relentless, forcing Tessa to summon every ounce of her stamina. She would not let him escape, not when another lifeless body lay cold and abandoned, adorned with a mocking symbol of frozen beauty.

Tessa's boots crunched through the snow, each step propelling her forward with unyielding determination. The woods were a labyrinth in the dim moonlight, but she kept pace, her eyes scanning the ground for signs of passage.

For one heart-stopping moment, the trail seemed to vanish. Tessa halted, her chest heaving as she searched for any clue, any indentation or disturbance that might reveal the path of their quarry. The snow lay pristine in a clearing ahead, untouched and deceptively calm. Her mind raced. This man was cunning, experienced enough to attempt a misdirect.

As the gap closed, the figure glanced back, a flicker of fear in his eyes that confirmed he knew this pursuit was not one he could outrun. With a burst of speed born from sheer adrenaline, Tessa lunged forward, her fingers grazing the back of the runner's jacket.

"Got you," she hissed under her breath.

Their collision was inevitable. And when they were upon one another, Tessa saw that the runner was indeed a man. In his sheer terror and desperation, he threw a punch as they fell—a punch that connected with Tessa's jaw. A normal person would have reeled from the impact, but Tessa merely blinked, unfazed, her condition rendering her impervious to the assault.

As she pinned him to the ground, she saw that he was about thirty, muscles honed not in a gym but through the kind of hard living that leaves scars deeper than skin. His eyes held a meanness that came from being cornered one too many times. She cataloged each detail of his behavior, her profiler's acumen dissecting his every move. His strength was formidable; sinewy muscles coiled and flexed beneath her grip, a testament to a life that had known physical toil. Yet, despite his brawn, there was a desperation in his actions, a frenetic energy that belied a deep-seated fear. He fought not just to escape but to evade a reckoning he knew was inevitable.

He grunted, trying to swing again. Tessa leaned back instinctively, and then planted a knee into his chest. He gasped, and all of the fight went out of him. His eyes wide, she withdrew her knee and rolled him over, locking his arms behind his back. She felt no real sense of triumph,, only the cold sense of duty as she stared down at the man who seemed to have killed and poorly disposed of Emily Radley.

Then, breaking through the sounds of exertion and the whisper of the wind, came the heavy footfalls of Jake approaching. His presence was a reassurance, a solid backup she had come to rely on without question. Tessa maintained her hold, leveraging her body weight to keep the suspect down as Jake loomed over them, his breath coming in measured gusts.

"Need a hand?" Jake quipped, though his voice carried the strain of their pursuit.

Together, they maneuvered the man upright, pressing his back against the rough bark of an old pine tree. Tessa's hands never wavered as Jake swiftly retrieved the handcuffs from his belt, the metallic click echoing through the silence like a gavel falling. They secured the suspect's wrists behind him, the steel bands a cold and unyielding symbol of their authority.

"No…please…" the man gasped. "I can explain…I can…"

"Good," Tessa said. "But for now, I'd like to get out of this snow. So shut up and walk."

"Look, I know I….shit, please, this is a mistake…"

Tessa wanted answers but she knew she'd not get any suitable, genuine answers until they were out of the woods and the suspect had caught his breath and had time to think. Besides…she was irritated that he'd made her run and didn't want her attitude to sway her judgement. So, with the suspect between them, Tessa and Jake made their way back to the pond, the police, and the dead, cold body of Emily Radley.

CHAPTER TWELVE

The clock on the precinct wall was just a few ticks away from 1:00 AM, as Tessa and Jake walked into the building. The polished linoleum of the floor gleamed as she strode through the maze of desks and cubicles near the center of the precinct. The air was thick with tension and the stale scent of coffee that failed to mask the undercurrent of adrenaline and sweat from officers who had been working double shifts.

Jake matched her pace as they advanced past the lowered gazes and hushed tones of detectives immersed in their own webs of crime and consequence. A murmur of respect threaded through the room at their passing; Tessa assumed they'd already earned that the man who'd just been brought in by Bowen and his men were apprehended by these visiting agents—and that they may very well have caught the killer.

They reached the door of the interrogation room, a nondescript slab of wood etched with scratches and the ghostly fingerprints of countless apprehended suspects. Bowen and one of his officers were waiting, both of them tense with anticipation.

"Can we get you anything?" Bowen asked.

"No, thanks," Tessa said.

"Just let us know if you need anything, then."

He gave a solemn little nod as Jake nudged open the door, allowing Tessa to enter first. The artificial light within spilled out into the dim corridor like an accusatory spotlight.

In the seventeen-minute drive to the precinct, Sheriff Bowen and his team had managed to get the bare basics on their suspect. He was Brent Fallen, and twenty-four-year-old screw up who had several dings on his record…all drug-related. He currently worked two jobs, one as a dishwasher at a local greasy spoon diner, and another at a car garage on the brink of going out of business. In high school, he'd played hokey and had been on the brink of going to college for it, but an injury had brought that to a stop.

In other words, he fit almost every angle of the profile Tessa had pieced together.

Inside the interrogation room, Brent Fallen sat cuffed to the table, a former athlete whose glory days were now just echoes in a hollow chamber of envy and bitterness. His posture was rigid, shoulders squared against the inevitability of the forthcoming confrontation. As Tessa's gaze fell upon him, she felt no pain, no empathy – only the clinical detachment honed by years of being an outlier in a world governed by sensations she could never grasp.

She did recall, though, the punch he'd doled out on her. She'd not felt the pain of it, but it had been a solid blow. She'd checked the bruise over in the car, the brown crescent that started on the right side of her chin and reached up to her lips.

"Mr. Fallen," Tessa began, her voice as steady as the pulse she knew beat somewhere beneath his layers of defiance. She'd already decided how she would start the interrogation…and it wasn't going to be with basic questioning. "I'd like you to take a look at something."

She slid a small evidence bag across the table, the contents catching the harsh light of the room. It was the snowflake pendant they'd found on Emily's neck, and now it lay between them, a silent symbol of mortality.

Brent's eyes were cold and unaffected. He looked at the necklace for about two seconds before directing his gaze back at Tessa. "What about it?" he asked.

"Have you ever seen this before?" Her eyes locked onto his, searching for any flicker of recognition, any telltale sign of guilt. Tessa was adept at reading people, at peeling back the layers to reveal the truth that others might miss in their own rush of emotions.

Brent's eyes darted down, glinting briefly with something that could have been dismissed as simple curiosity by the untrained observer. But Tessa was far from untrained, and she cataloged the reaction with clinical precision.

"Never seen it in my life," Brent replied, but there was a tightness in his voice, a defensive quality that clung to the syllables and imbued them with more weight than the words alone would carry.

"Think carefully, Mr. Fallen," Jake interjected, his tone offering a stark contrast to Tessa's, warm yet edged with the steel of authority. "This was on Emily's neck. Being honest here can only help you."

"Emily," Brent said. "Emily Radley…the woman you think I apparently killed, right?"

"That's where we are at the moment, yes," Jake said. "So answer the question. *Have you seen this before?*"

"I already answered that question."

“And that’s the answer you’re sticking to?” Jake asked.

The room seemed to shrink around them, the walls closing in as the gravity of the situation settled over Brent Fallen like a shroud. The silence stretched taut, filled with unspoken accusations and the echoes of questions yet to be asked.

Brent Fallen's chair scraped against the sterile linoleum as he leaned forward, muscles taut beneath the orange fabric of his jumpsuit. The air in the interrogation room grew thick, charged with a hostility that buzzed like a live wire exposed. His eyes, dark and piercing, fixed upon Tessa with an intensity that belied the calm she embodied.

"Are you deaf or just stupid?" Brent sneered, his voice a blade sharpened by fury. "I said I haven't seen the damned thing before."

Tessa felt a flutter in her chest—a response not to fear but to surprise. In all her years, few had dared to direct such naked aggression toward her, and none had done so without regretting it. Yet here was Brent Fallen, rage radiating from him in waves, setting a new bar for defiance. If he was truly sticking by his story of innocence, he was going about it the wrong way.

"Mr. Fallen," Tessa began, her tone even, betraying no hint of the alarm that had momentarily flickered within her. "Hostility won't serve you here. Cooperation might."

She studied him, noting the way his jaw set, the pulse that ticked visibly at his throat. He was like a cornered animal, lashing out in desperation rather than calculated malice. It was a reaction she'd seen before, but never one so raw, so visceral. She could also see something like wisdom back there, something telling him it would be foolish to show his ass in this particular setting.

"Fine," he spat, slumping back into his chair with a huff that sent a cold draught skittering across the metal table between them. "What do you want from me?"

Jake, who'd been observing silently, stepped in. "We want to understand, Brent. Why were you out there in the woods tonight? And if you're innocent, why did you run when you saw us?"

The question hung in the air, a challenge wrapped in the guise of inquiry. Tessa watched Brent's face closely, looking for the cracks in his armor. Her mind, sharp and unyielding, dissected his every micro-expression, sifting through them for the truth.

"Wasn't doing anything wrong," Brent muttered, but his gaze shifted, darting away from theirs. "Just out for a walk, is all."

"At midnight? In the middle of winter?" Tessa pressed, her voice calm but insistent. "Without any sort of clear, defined path where you were standing?"

"Your story doesn't add up, and running from law enforcement only makes you look guilty," Jake said.

"Guilty? You think I'm scared of you?" Brent's laugh was hollow, mocking. "I ran because I don't trust cops. Not after what you people did to my brother."

The mention of his brother—another piece of the puzzle—resonated with Tessa. She knew the history, the narratives that unfolded in smaller communities where trust in law enforcement was the first casualty. Empathy was a tool in her arsenal, one she wielded with precision.

"Well, whatever that particular story may be, Agent Sullivan and I aren't part of it," Tessa said.

"Yeah, feds," Brent said, rolling his eyes. "That's *so* much better."

"Well, trust has to start somewhere, Tessa said. "Let it start now," she offered, her gaze unwavering.

Silence fell once more, a silent arbiter waiting to see which side would give way under its pressure. Tessa held Brent's gaze, unflinching, willing him to see reason through the fog of his anger.

"What are you…a Hallmark card writer?" Brent said.

Tessa's eyes narrowed as she watched the realization dawn on Brent's face. The interrogation room was stark, the fluorescent lights casting a clinical glow over the cold metal table that stood between them.

"Three murders, Brent," Tessa said slowly, her voice barely louder than a whisper but slicing through the tension like a blade. "Emily Radley, just another victim to you?"

"Wait—three?" Brent's voice cracked, his facade crumbling as he leaned forward, his cuffed hands gripping the edge of the table. "Not just this Radley girl?"

"Nope. Three. All within the course of a week."

A bit of fear worked its way into Brent's expression, and suddenly, a lot of the venom seemed to seep right out of him. "You think I did all that?"

The shift in his demeanor was palpable; the aggressive posturing had ebbed away, leaving behind a flicker of fear in his eyes. She knew this was a turning point, one that could unravel the knots of the case or tighten them further.

"Gary called me, alright?" Brent blurted out, and Tessa could almost hear the clang of the truth as it hit the table. "I was supposed to meet him at that pond."

"Who's Gary?" Tessa asked.

"The Radley chick's boyfriend. Gary Hutchins. He wanted coke for him and Emily. Just a little party in the woods, I think."

"So you *knew* Emily Radley?" Jake said.

"I knew *of* her. But I know Gary pretty well. I, um…" He paused here but then seemed to understand that what he was about to admit to was far less damning than what he was being accused of. "I've been selling to him for about a year."

"Cocaine?"

"Yeah."

"We already searched you, though," Jake pointed out. "If you were out there to sell, that opens up a whole batch of other questions. For starters…where are the drugs?"

"I ditched them when I started running. You have to understand, man…I thought you were chasing me down because of the dealing…not that you thought I'd killed someone."

"Okay," Tessa said. "Then why come through the woods instead of just pulling up in your car to meet them?"

"Because the cops have been all over the place lately, and I wanted to be able to get away quick. Dealing to Gary s one thing but…a lot of people respected Emily, you know? And I guess now that I know there have been three women killed, the police presence makes sense."

"So you walked all that way through the woods?" Jake asked, still not convinced.

"It's not so far. There's an old hunting road behind my house that bends out that way. It's only like a fifteen-minute walk from my back door to that pond.

Tessa could feel the lead unraveling, could feel Brent Fallen leading them to yet another dead end.

"Look, I never touched Emily Radley," Brent went on, desperation seeping into his tone. "I swear to you, I just brought what Gary asked for. That's it. I'm no killer."

Tessa let his words hang in the air for a moment, measuring their weight against the evidence they had gathered so far. She glanced at Jake, who gave a subtle nod, indicating he too felt the shift in the narrative.

"Go on," she urged, her voice still quiet, commanding.

Brent sucked in a breath, his chest rising and falling rapidly. "I was walking through the woods, taking the path I always take, when I saw cop cars through the trees." His voice hitched as he relived the memory. "Lights flashing, cutting through the night like...like warning signals. I froze and got scared."

"How long had you been standing there before we started chasing you?"

"I don't know. Maybe like a minute, Two at most. I was trying to figure out what the hell was going on down there at the pond."

"So you're saying you didn't even know there was a body?"

"No. Not until you told me before we got to the pond."

Tessa sat back, letting the pieces fall into place. Brent's revelation painted a new picture—one where fear, not guilt, fueled his flight. She thought about the foot chase, the panic in Brent's steps as he stumbled through the snow, a man trying to outrun suspicion itself.

"Alright, Brent," she said finally. "We'll need to verify your story. Every detail."

"Check with Gary!" Brent exclaimed, relief washing over him as he realized they might believe him. "He'll tell you the same."

Tessa nodded, her mind already racing ahead, piecing together timelines and motives. They would check with Gary, corroborate Brent's alibi. Of course, Gary—who she'd only know as *Emily's boyfriend* until now—was dealing with a huge loss. He'd found his girlfriend dead, already interrogated by local PD.

But something else tugged at her—a detail, a sound from that night in the woods that didn't fit.

"I need you to think hard about this next question," she said. "While you were out there in those woods, did you happen to see anyone else?"

As he thought about it, Tessa realized that all of the fire had gone out of him. Now, he simply seemed relieved that he was no longer being grilled for the murder of three young women.

"No... but," he hesitated, and when he continued, his voice was a notch lower, "but I'm pretty sure I heard someone else."

"Someone else?" Jake prompted, narrowing his eyes at Brent.

"Yeah," Brent swallowed hard. "When I was on my down to meet Gary, I thought I heard footsteps off in the distance...maybe some branches snapping. But I figured it might just be deer, you know? I really didn't think much of it."

Tessa's heart skipped, and for a moment, she could almost hear the phantom footsteps Brent described, feel the chill of the night air whispering secrets among the trees.

“Where were you before you went into the woods?” she asked. “Tell us about your night.”

He did, and he did so with great detail, making sure they knew he was not the man they were looking for. He told them how he'd worked at the diner until 10:30, then went straight to his girlfriend's house, where he had a few beers with some friends. He left there, went home, and then headed straight into the woods with the coke he'd intended to sell to Gary.

"Alright," Tessa said, her voice steady, though her mind raced with the implications. She made a mental note of all of this, now all but certain Brent was not their man. “We’ll need the names of the people you were hanging out with before heading out to the pond.”

“Absolutely.”

He gave them gladly, along with phone numbers and where each of them worked. And as she watched Jake type the information into the Notes app on his phone, Tessa couldn’t deny the sting of disappointment. Somehow, yet again, a lead that had seemed so solid had become nothing…and their killer remained just as intangible as the frigid cold outside.

Worse than that, she knew what had to come next. More grieving parents, more sorrow and an inability to provide those heartbroken people with any answers.

CHAPTER THIRTEEN

"God, I hate this part."

Tessa said this out loud as she looked to the house to her right. Jake, at the steering wheel, followed her gaze. The Radley home loomed at the end of a desolate cul-de-sac, its facade a stark contrast against the overcast sky. A solitary police cruiser sat in the driveway, like a sentinel standing guard over the manicured lawn.

They got out of the car together and walked up the sidewalk in silence. She knew that the cop here with the Radleys had already broken the news, but it would still be fresh. Less than an hour had passed since these poor people had been told their daughter was dead.

As Tessa and Jake approached the front door, it cracked open before they could knock. Sheriff Bowen was on the other side, his face etched with the grim news he'd recently delivered.

"Agent Flint, Agent Sullivan," he nodded somberly, stepping aside to let them enter.

Tessa's gaze swept the interior, a picturesque suburban sanctuary now fractured by tragedy. Polished wood floors and high, crown-molded ceiling snow felt like the interior of a tomb. From somewhere further back, down a wide hall that seemed to end in a dining room, Tessa could hear soft, murmured conversation.

"How long ago did you tell them?" Jake asked Bowen.

"Twenty minutes. The father is in shock. So much so that I've called for an ambulance. There's a sister on the way over, but for now the mother is hanging in there. Wrecked, obviously, but able to talk."

"Thanks, Sheriff," Tessa said.

"I'll be looking the place over while you speak to them. Just holler if you need anything."

The sheriff's departure left behind a silence that seemed to pulse with the weight of unsaid words, the air thick with the scent of sorrow that no amount of floral wallpaper or family portraits could mask. Tessa and Jake followed the sound of hushed talking and found the Radleys in the dining room. They were huddled together at the end of the table, the wife having wrapped an arm around her husband. Bowen hadn't been over-exaggerating: Mr. Radley was in shock. His eyes were unblinking, and he was rocking slowly back and forth.

"Mr. and Mrs. Radley?" Tessa ventured, her voice steady despite the heaviness pressing down on the room.

Mrs. Radley looked up from the frozen state of her husband's face. She clutched a tissue, her eyes red-rimmed and lost in the kind of pain that words could never reach. But there was no reply from Mr. Radley at all. The poor man was simply disconnected from everything, untethered from the world by grief.

"Mrs. Radley," Tessa began, taking a seat across from the grief-stricken woman. "I know this is an incredibly difficult time, but anything you can share about Emily could help us find who did this. If you can't manage right now, we can come back later, but right now, time is really of the essence."

Mrs. Radley took a shuddering breath, her voice barely above a whisper. "She was our star... always so driven, so full of life." She faltered, the enormity of her loss threatening to engulf her.

"Did she have any problems with anyone? Or maybe incidents that worried her?" Jake added softly, his experience with loss lending empathy to his inquiry.

"Emily never mentioned anything like that to us. But even if there were such a thing…she was always so happy. So damned happy, almost to the point of being naïve."

“Did you know any of her friends well?” Tessa asked. She wasn’t going to mention Gary because of what they’d learned about Gary and their daughter earlier in the night—that they’d planned on hooking up out in the woods, waiting on a drug dealer. It just wasn’t the sort of thing you told parents about their kid in the moments following their murder.

"We didn't know all her friends,” Mrs. Radley replied. “John?” she asked, looking to her husband with sad, hopeful eyes, trying to break through to him. “John, do you recall any of Emily’s friends ever coming around?"

His only response was a subtle nod, so small that it was barely even there at all. His eyes remained distant, as if he were searching for some sign of his daughter in the room around them.

“I’m sorry,” Mrs. Radley said, choking back a sob. “I don’t feel like I’m being very much help…”

Tessa felt the hardwood floor creak under her weight as she shifted uneasily, the sound a stark reminder of the fragility pervading the

Radley household. She observed Mrs. Radley dab at her eyes with a tissue that had long since given up on serving its purpose.

"You're doing the best you can," Tessa said sympathetically. "I have more questions…is that okay?"

"Yes. Please. I want to help."

"The location where she was found by her boyfriend…that pond. Is it a place she usually went? Sheriff Bowen tells us locals sometimes ice skated there when the water was frozen over."

"Oh, yes. It was…it was the pond where she first learned to skate. Where she broke her first ankle, where she nearly fell through the ice, where…" She stopped, and her entire face contorted into a mask of pain and loss. After a gut-wrenching moan, she managed to push on." She trained every day, rain or shine. But that pond was where it began. And I think she still went out there every now and then just for the nostalgia of it…to remember where she'd come from."

Among other reasons, Tessa thought with a sting of guilt.

"Was there anyone who might have resented her success?" Jake asked. "Anyone she competed against who took things too personally?"

A shadow passed over Mrs. Radley's face, as if contemplating a darker side of her daughter's ambition she hadn't considered. "Emily never mentioned anything like that. So I really don't know. I *do* know that there have been two competitions she won where the runner-up sought her out for advice. But that's about it."

"What about Gary?" Tessa asked. "Do you think he might have had something against her?"

"Oh Lord, no. That boy worshipped Emily. He…well, Sheriff Bowen said he's at the station…that the Poor boy got sick at one point from the crying."

Tessa nodded, filing away each piece of information like evidence in a case file. She knew Gary had been interrogated by a few cops, but she wondered if maybe she and Jake needed to speak with him as well. But it wasn't just the facts of the case that occupied her thoughts—it was the gnawing idea that they were all connected by something sinister.

As Mrs. Radley continued to reminisce about Emily, Tessa's mind began to drift, piecing together the fragments of a puzzle only she could see. The other victims, like Emily, had been young, vibrant, successful in their own right. Each one an embodiment of potential that seemed to scream out to some twisted soul driven by jealousy.

"One last question, and we'll leave you alone for now," Tessa asked. She pulled up a picture of the snowflake pendant on her phone and showed it to Mrs. Radley. “Do you happen to know if Emily owned this necklace?”

She shook her head sadly. “I don’t know. What I *can* tell you is that Emily rarely wore jewelry. I…I don’t know if that helps.”

“It does. Now, if you—”

She was interrupted by the sudden and unexpected voice of Mr. Radley. His eyes were no longer distant; they stared directly into Tessa with fire and anger, but also a lot of pain.

"Find who did this to our girl," he said. There was venom in his voice, something close to hatred. “Find who did this and make him pay.”

“We intend to,” Jake said.

“Mrs. Radley, how long had Emily been living in Rhode Island?”

“About a year and a half.”

“And why did she move?”

“Well, she was going to college for two years but dropped out when she realized she didn’t have time for college *and* training. She then got a job as a skating instructor, so she just stayed down there.”

“And Sheriff Bowen tells us she was in town to visit you, right?”

“Well, us and Gary. Yes.”

“Does she still have a room here?”

“She does. Head back down the hall, take a right off the stairs, and hers is the second room down that hall. Help yourself.”

“Thank you.”

She and Jake stepped away from the table and out of the dining room. As they went back through the hall and toward the stairs, she saw Sheriff Bowen heading through the front door. Outside, an ambulance had pulled up quietly and discreetly—a reminder that Bowen had called one for Mr. Radley.

They followed Mrs. Radley's directions and found Emily's old room without any trouble. Tessa stepped into the room and found that although its former resident no longer lived there, it still spoke volumes of the life once brimming within its four walls. Tessa got the impression that this had been done by Emily's parents keeping a sort of playful museum for their daughter. Trophies and medals adorned shelves, each gleaming under the soft glow of a desk lamp, their presence a testament to a discipline that demanded every ounce of Emily's waking hours. Posters of figure skating icons wallpapered the room, proof that a young girl with big dreams had once lived here.

But there were also signs of the present day. A small suitcase and backpack were leaning against the far wall. A hoodie was tossed on the foot of the bed. A tube of Chapstick and a hairbrush sat on the edge of the bedside table—indicators of Emily's recent stay with her parents.

Tessa moved with reverence, her leather boots sinking into the plush carpet as she perused the collection of accolades. The scent of lavender hung in the air, mingling with the sharper tang of sorrow that seemed to seep from the very walls. She could almost hear the echo of blades slicing through ice, the breathless cheers of a crowd, the heartbeat of competition thrumming through the room.

It was far too similar to Elana Dean's room…so similar that it sent a chill through Tessa.

"This is eerie, huh?" Jake asked, apparently having noticed her unease.

"Our killer certainly has a type," she said. "Jesus, Jake…are we going to have to reach out to every winter athlete in the state to warn them?"

She'd said it in jest but the idea did have some traction. And if it came to that, this entire case was going to get so much messier.

However, before Jake had the opportunity to respond, Tessa's phone vibrated in her pocket, jarring them both.

"This is Agent Flint," she answered.

"Agent Flint, it's Officer Garcia from forensics," came the voice on the other end. Envisioning Garcia took her back to the start of this case, back before they knew how deep and tense it was truly going to get.

"Hello. Do you have something new for us?"

"Maybe. We've tracked down two online sellers of those snowflake pendants. We sort of had to because no one local sells anything like that. There were a few that were close at the gift shops in the ski resorts, but nothing was an exact match. But these two online sellers…yeah, they're spot-on matches. One of them says they just shipped out a bulk order—to an address only thirty minutes away from my labs."

A pulse of electricity shot down Tessa's spine. This was the break they needed—a tangible lead they could follow. More than that, it seemed like a direct hit. She glanced around the room once more, at the life interrupted, and felt a renewed sense of purpose.

With a quiet nod to herself, Tessa confirmed the details with Garcia and ended the call, her mind already racing with the possibilities of what lay ahead.

"Got a lead?" Jake asked, noting the intense look on her face.

"Someone's ordered a bulk shipment of those pendants online," Tessa replied, her mind working like a steel trap, piecing together fragments of information, seeking patterns. "Garcia traced it to an address not far from here."

"Seems like a smoking gun to me," Jake said.

Tessa nodded, and they hurried out of the room. As they hurried to excuse themselves, Tessa thought their hurried footsteps sounded like heartbeats within the house. She felt the chase tighten around her heart—an ominous drumbeat propelling them forward.

CHAPTER FOURTEEN

"John Smith," Jake said. "*That's* the name we've got to go on?"

"That's the name the package was sent to, Tessa said. "A third-party seller, not anyone like Amazon."

"Clearly a fake name, right? Is that the vibe you're getting?"

"Probably."

She glared out into the darkness as Jake drove through the night. The address was taking them down another secondary road, mostly leveled out and smooth but offering up the occasional patches of gravel as the road led them back into the forests. The dashboard clock read 3:28 and though Tessa knew exhaustion would claim her eventually, her mind and heart weren't concerned with such things as they neared the address Officer Garcia had given them.

Another five minutes passed before Jake brought the car to their destination. As Jake turned into what appeared to be only the memory of a driveway, the headlights washed over the façade of a dilapidated cabin nestled in the heart of the forest. It felt like a different planet, but it was only about fifteen miles from where Elana Dean's life had been brutally snuffed out.

The address, linked to a John Smith—a name as common as it was suspicious—was their fragile tether to unraveling a murderer's design. Tessa's mind, usually a fortress against distractions, couldn't help but wander to the grief-stricken faces of Emily Radley's parents. Their despair was palpable, a stark reminder that time was slipping through their fingers like grains of sand.

"Looks like we're here," Jake muttered, his voice cutting through her reverie. His breath fogged up the window momentarily, a ghostly imprint that faded as fast as it appeared.

Tessa nodded, her expression unreadable. She stepped out of the car, senses sharpening to the nocturnal whispers of the forest. The air was bitingly cold, a frigid reminder of the season. Despite her inability to feel pain, she *could* feel temperature shifts such as hot and cold. In fact, there were times when she thought she may feel those sensations more than anyone else. Right now, the chill didn't bother her but she knew if she stood out in it for an extended period of time, it would sink into her deeply.

They swept their gazes over the cabin, its windows dark, the front door looking as if it hadn't bene opened it ages. Shadows clung to it like desperate secrets, the wooden planks of the porch groaned under the weight of neglect. No smoke curled from the chimney; no light flickered within to ward off intruders or to beacon the lost.

"It looks abandoned," Tessa observed. Her voice low, carrying a weight that seemed to disturb the silence around them. The place didn't just seem empty; it felt hollow, as though it had been holding its breath for years, waiting for this very moment of discovery.

"Can't be if it had something delivered here," Jake pointed out. "Maybe there's just nobody home."

"Or they don't want visitors at this hour," Tessa added, allowing herself a moment of dry humor despite the gravity of their situation. They both knew what was at stake. Every second that ticked by could mean the difference between life and death, justice and impunity.

Silently, they circled the cabin, peering through windows clouded by time and dirt. The yard was unremarkable, a flat and mostly dead expanse of land, dotted by tall, bold trees that blended in with all of the ones surrounding then. The stillness was oppressive, wrapping around Tessa like a shroud. This was a place of endings, she thought grimly, and they were about to peel back the curtain on a killer's act.

After making a loop of the property, they finally climbed the porch steps. Tessa's hand hovered near the rusted doorknob, her fingers coiled into a hesitant fist. The night emitted a silence so thick it felt like a physical barrier, one she was about to break with a single, decisive action. She knocked, the sound like a bomb in the woods, but there was no answer—not that she'd been expecting one. She then tried opening it, unsurprised to find it locked.

"This place is a tomb," Jake said. "I feel like we could just sort of help ourselves, you know?"

"Breaking and entering," she murmured, the frost in the air making each word a visible puff of conflict. "It doesn't sit right."

"Neither does the murder of three young women," Jake said, his tone bitter. "You know as well as I do that the lines between right and wrong get blurry in the face of duty." He started walking down the porch steps, heading for the car.

"What are you doing?"

"Getting a lock-pic set."

She knew it was the right decision—that it needed to be done. She wasn't exactly a stickler for the rules herself, but this seemed like a bold and important choice.

She said nothing else as Jake came back from the car with the small vinyl kit. As he worked in the old lock, she watched the moonlight play off the metallic tools in Jake's hands.

"Think of it as an unwelcome invitation," Jake said, a wry smile touching his lips. He inserted the tension wrench into the lock, feeling for the familiar click of tumblers yielding to his touch.

Tessa's jaw clenched, her mind racing through the potential consequences of their choice. Yet, deep down, she knew they had already made the decision the moment they stepped onto the property. There was no turning back now—not when lives hung in the balance, not when justice for Elana Dean, Rachel Coolidge and Emily Radley teetered on a knife's edge.

With a soft snick, the lock gave way, surrendering its secrets to them. Jake pushed open the door, and Tessa's senses were instantly assaulted by the musty smell of neglect. The cabin greeted them with shadows and silence, a tableau of abandonment that sent a shiver crawling up her spine.

Inside, the absence of life was palpable. No hum of electricity, no babble of running water—just the oppressive quiet of a place long forgotten by the world. Tessa tried the light switch on the wall by the front door, but there was no power. They navigated through the darkness, Tessa removing her small flashlight from her coat pocket and swept the beam across the room, illuminating the sad remnants of human occupancy.

An old sleeping bag lay sprawled in a corner. Only, maybe it wasn't so old; it didn't show the fade or wear of age. It wasn't new, but she didn't think it had been there for long. Empty food containers were scattered haphazardly, a testament to the transient presence of someone seeking refuge—or something more sinister. Tessa's eyes lingered on a crushed water bottle, the label peeling away from the plastic like the shedding skin of some slumbering beast.

"Someone's been here," Jake whispered, his voice barely rising above the stillness. "Recently enough."

"The fairly new sleeping bag agrees with you." Tessa commented.

"Too bad they didn't leave us a welcome note," Jake said.

Tessa's gaze followed the beam of her flashlight as it danced over discarded wrappers and dust-laden surfaces, searching for any clue that might connect this forsaken place to the horrors they were chasing.

The chill in the air seemed to seep into her bones, as if the cabin itself resented their intrusion. This was more than just an empty shell in the woods—it was a silent witness to the unseen monster they were hunting. And somewhere within these walls, she hoped to find the whisper of a lead that would bring them closer to the truth.

The cabin consisted of only four rooms, including the large, open space that served as the living room, dining room, and kitchen. Aside from the dust, dirt, and rat droppings, the large, open space was empty. The other three rooms consisted of two small bedrooms and an even smaller bathroom. The bathroom smelled faintly of urine, but the scent of age and neglect was stronger.

To the right of the kitchen, a small door was partially opened. Tessa walked over to it and shone her flashlight down into it. A set of stairs led down into the darkness.

"We don't have the best luck with basements," Jack said as Tessa started down them.

"I'm choosing to ignore that for right now."

Tessa descended the rickety wooden steps and found that they led into a cellar. The air grew heavier, thick with the musty scent of damp earth and decay. Her flashlight beam led them down the narrow stairs, unveiling the secrets that lay dormant below.

The cellar was a hollow cavity in the belly of the forest, its very existence an ominous pit that threatened to swallow them whole. A few wooden shelves lined the walls, but they stood barren, save for the occasional cobweb that clung to the corners like cotton candy spun from nightmares. But it wasn't the emptiness that captured Tessa's attention—it was what lay scattered across the dirt floor.

"Over here," she called out, kneeling by a few scraps of paper—what looked like old tears from magazine or newspapers. Basic computer print-puts were present, too. Like the sleeping bag above, they didn't seem very old. These had not been here for very long. The pieces from a magazine still held a glossy sheen. As Jake approached from behind with his own flashlight, Tessa gingerly lifted a page, bringing it closer to her light.

"Looks like they're form magazine articles," she said. However, because there were only portions of the pages, she wasn't able to get a full story.

What she did see, though, were names.

"I'll be damned," she said as her eyes scanned the words, some of them ripped. The first two names she saw were unfamiliar. "Lila Greene... and here, Marissa Vale," she said, reading out loud. "And on this one," she said, holding up an edge to an old scrap of newspaper. "Elana Dean."

"Any dates or other info?" Jake asked his brow furrowed as he scrutinized the scraps.

"None that I see," Tessa replied, frustration edging her voice. "I think these were accidentally left behind—just scraps for a much bigger collection." And as she said that, she saw a portion of another name, interrupted by a rip along the edge of the paper.

...to keep their eyes on up-and-comer Rachel Cooli—

"What the hell is this?" Jake asked.

But the answer was clear to both of them. In the chill silence that settled between the creaks of the old house above, that this dank and dreary place had harbored evil. Yet the killer had been meticulous, leaving behind no tangible threads to follow, only the hollowed husks of his past presence.

"Let's keep looking," Tessa suggested, rising to her feet, feeling the weight of dust motes dancing in the stagnant air around her. They sifted through the rest, touching upon each discarded piece of paper, each fragment of what used to be, hoping for a lead.

But as the minutes dragged on, the hope dimmed like the weakening light of her flashlight. There was nothing else here—no overlooked evidence, no real clues.

"We'll call Bowen and maybe even Lawson," she said. "Get a forensics team out here to see if they can pull hair or prints."

Her mind whirred with the implications of their find—or rather, the lack of it. The killer was a shadow, a phantom adept at eluding capture. To know they were standing where he had likely stood at one point was both chilling and infuriating.

With a final, lingering glance at the cellar's gloom, Tessa turned away, the beam of her flashlight leading them back towards the stairs. They emerged from the bowels of the earth, leaving behind the cold embrace of the dark, their search futile but their determination unyielded. The mystery of the cabin in the woods remained just that—a mystery, veiled and unsolved.

Before leaving, Tessa took out her phone. The reception out in the woods wasn't the best, so the connection as she pulled up her browser was slow. Still, she typed in the two new names they'd found on the papers in the cellar.

She typed in the first name, Lila Greene. The results revealed that she was a journalist who followed winter sports very closely. Out of

Bangor, she focused on skiing and figure skating specifically, with an almost obsessive quality.

She then typed in the second name, Marissa Vale. She was a thirty-year-old downhill skier who'd nearly made the Olympics on two occasions.

"Look at this," she said as they neared the door. A journalist and a downhill skier."

"The journalist doesn't really fit the case, does it?" Jake said.

"Maybe not. But if this *is*—or used to be—the killer's lair and we found her name, she should be warned. As for Marissa Vale, we need to put her under surveillance."

"Good," Jake said. "That gives us a reason to get the hell out of here."

"You drive," she said. "Maybe back to the hotel. We need to some sleep. But on the way, I'll call the PD and then the bureau…get some eyes and patrols on Greene and Vale."

They left the cabin again, walking out into the dark. The purples and pinks of dawn were still an hour and a half away. Tessa tried to view it as her and Jake getting an early start, but, in all reality, she wasn't sure she'd ever felt so far behind.

CHAPTER FIFTEEN

He was humming a song as he descended the creaking wooden stairs into his sanctuary. Something from the 80s that he couldn't' quite place, one of those earworms that seemed relentless. A single naked bulb hung from the ceiling, casting a jaundiced glow over the room that had become a shrine to his twisted obsession.

The basement was a cavernous space, concealed beneath the innocuous facade of suburbia, where no one would think to look for the macabre gallery he had painstakingly curated. He had another area off in the woods, a forgotten cabin that he'd moved away from once he realized there was a thick police presence in the area.

What the hell had he been thinking, having the pendants delivered through the mail?

No matter. He'd moved, left no trace evidence, and he still had work to do.

He moved through the cramped quarters with a sense of reverence, brushing past the relics of his fixation. His eyes, sharp and alert despite the dim light, scanned the walls plastered with of triumph. First, there were the headlines from local papers. Elana had come first, and he had a few different papers reporting on her murder. Only one had picked up Rachel's murder because it only happened about thirty-eight hours ago. And it would be at least another day before any local papers printed anything about Emily.

Still, scant or not, he was quite proud of it. Was it foolish to hang such things from the walls? Yes, of course. But it was also a huge encouragement to him—a reminder of how well he'd done.

But he had photos, too. Things he'd found online and even picked up at live events where he'd watched and scouted his victims. The photographs showcased the brightest smiles of female athletes frozen in their moments of glory—on podiums, crossing finish lines, holding trophies aloft. These women had been the darlings of the sporting world, their faces beaming with the kind of success that had always eluded him. Their images formed a grotesque mosaic, a constellation of stars whose light he had extinguished one by one.

His fingertips grazed the edges of a frame, tracing the outline of a skier caught mid-jump, her form perfect against a backdrop of snow and sky. The killer's breath hitched ever so slightly, a quiet sound swallowed by the stillness of the lair. He lingered on the image, absorbing the details—the bend of her knees, the poise in her posture, the sheer audacity of flight—and felt a surge of something akin to admiration, or perhaps envy.

In this clandestine chamber, removed from the scrutiny of the world above, he allowed himself a moment of reflection. With each piece of memorabilia, he had claimed a fragment of their excellence, their vitality. It was a collection borne of darkness, yes, but also a tribute to the light they once held—a light he believed was now his alone to possess.

He turned away from the wall, his silhouette merging with the shadows as he made his way to a worn desk in the corner of the room. There, amid the clutter of his lair, were more of the necklaces.

His fingers trembled slightly, the cool metal of the snowflake pendant palpable against his rough skin. Shadows clung to his form like a second skin, obscuring his features in the dim light of the basement lair. He turned the pendant over in his hand, its pattern identical to those he'd left on his victims—a signature of sorts, a chilling hallmark of his twisted achievements.

He stood motionless, save for the rhythmic caress of the pendant, as if each stroke could somehow link him to the vitality and prowess his victims had once embodied. The silence was total, save for the faint whisper of silver against skin. The cluttered room, festooned with the trophies of his obsession, seemed to hold its breath, complicit in the sanctity of his ritual.

The killer's gaze drifted across the room, alighting on the faces of smiling female athletes frozen in time, each one an epitome of strength and success that now haunted these four walls. Their eyes seemed to watch him from their frames, silent witnesses to the grim theater he had orchestrated.

His attention caught on one picture in particular, a photograph pinned amongst the many. It was out of place among the others; he was well aware of this. But it also felt *right.*

The photo depicted a younger version of himself, clad in hockey gear, mid-stride on the ice with a look of fierce determination etched into his youthful features. The memory surged forth unbidden—a high school game, the sharp crack of his knee giving out, the searing pain, and the immediate knowledge that his dreams were irreparably shattered.

For a moment, he was transported back to that frigid rink, the scent of cold sweat and the sound of blades slicing the ice vivid in his mind. His jaw clenched as the bitterness of that long-ago injury rose like bile. That injury had not only stolen his future; it had robbed him of recognition, of potential glory that should have been his. He'd had a promising future for a moment, but after one single second of misfortune, that had all been taken away.

With a shuddering breath, he tore his gaze from the photograph. The pendant lay in his palm, a physical reminder of the power he had seized through his macabre acts. Now, it was not the agony of a ruined knee that consumed him but a resolve steeled by resentment and an unquenchable thirst for the success he believed was owed to him.

Turning back to the room, he allowed the darkness to envelop him once more, the shadows conspiring with his malice. There, considering his stifled triumphs, he prepared to embark on yet another hunt—to claim another victory in the only way he knew how. He ignored the pendants for now and, instead, turned his attention to the small laptop.

The dim glow of the laptop screen cast eerie shadows across his face as he navigated to a video website. Each video he had bookmarked and watched over and over again was a benchmark of someone else's triumph, a moment in time where they had reached the pinnacle of success—a height he would never know.

With a deliberate click, Rachel Coolidge appeared on the screen, her form cutting through the snow with a grace and ferocity that seemed almost otherworldly. The video showed her descent down the mountain, her body in perfect harmony with the board beneath her feet as she shattered records and expectations alike. The killer watched intently, fixating on the way her muscles flexed and relaxed with each maneuver, the exuberant smile breaking across her features as she crossed the finish line. He could almost feel the rush of cold air against his skin, the vicarious thrill of victory—yet it was soured by the knowledge that it wasn't his to claim.

With a flick of the mouse, the scene shifted to Emily Radley, gliding over ice with the elegance of a swan taking to water. Her every pivot and leap was a symphony of motion, captivating and effortless. The crowd's roar exploded as she executed her final spin, landing with such precision that even the judges couldn't conceal their awe. The killer watched, transfixed, yet his eyes held none of the admiration one might expect. Instead, they were cold and calculating, as if dissecting the very essence of her talent.

A dark satisfaction curled at the corners of his mouth as the memories took a sinister turn. He could recall the precise moment when he had extinguished Rachel's vibrant flame, how the shock in her eyes flourished when she realized that her end would not be a blaze of glory but a silent snuffing out in the dead of night. His heart rate quickened as he remembered the weight of the snowflake pendant in his hands, its chill a stark contrast to the warmth of her life ebbing away.

Similarly, Emily's demise played back in his mind with grotesque clarity. She had been so confident, so full of life—until he'd showed her just how fragile and unextraordinary she truly was. He reveled in these recollections, believing that with each life taken, he absorbed a fragment of their achievements, their vitality. In his twisted mind, their murders were not just acts of violence but a transfer of power, a way for him to own the success that fate had denied him.

He leaned back in his chair, allowing himself a moment of perverse pride. These women, who had once soared so high, were now nothing more than trophies in his macabre collection. And as their images flickered and faded on the laptop screen, he felt a surge of anticipation for the next name to be added to his grim gallery.

He could feel the adrenaline beginning to surge through his veins as he contemplated his next move.

Rising from the chair, the killer paced the cramped space, each step deliberate. He passed the cluttered workbench, its surface littered with tools and trinkets,. But his attention was drawn back to an untouched, pristine snowflake pendant, identical to the ones found with Rachel, Elana, and Emily. It lay there, deceptively innocent, waiting to be claimed by its future bearer.

He picked up the pendant, rolling it between his thumb and forefinger, feeling the edges bite into his skin. It was a tangible connection to his next target, a binding contract signed in secrecy and silence. He would bestow it upon her just as he had the others, a final gift before taking everything else away.

CHAPTER SIXTEEN

As Jake drove them through a blanket of night that was just starting to break apart, Tessa could feel the first true signs of weariness settling in. She had no issues staying up for extended periods of time, but after about thirty hours, her body started to demand some rest. She felt it now, as Jack got them closer to the hotel.

"You know," Jake said. "A journalist obsessed with the topic could be a decent suspect, too."

"How so?"

"A journalist focused primarily on winter sports. If you follow something that closely and make it the core of your life's work, you'd be pretty damned knowledgeable about it, right? You'd know details about the athletes that others may not. You would come close to a sort of fanaticism, right?"

"Maybe. So, are you saying you think we should view Lily Greene as a suspect?"

"I think anyone not ruled out completely should be a suspect," he said. "Speaking of which, I don't think we should be letting Gary off the hook yet, either."

Oh yeah, Tessa thought. *Emily Radley's boyfriend.* The last twelve hours or so had been such a whirlwind that she'd forgotten that they had yet to speak with him.

As for Jake's point about Lily Greene, she had to admit…it did sort of fit the profile, albeit an incomplete one. Something about the relentless pursuit of cold, of speed, of victory—it mirrored the meticulous nature of the crimes, each executed with a precision that left little behind but sorrow.

The hotel's exterior lights cast a pallid glow over the sedan as Jake finally rolled it into the parking lot Tessa sat rigid in the passenger seat, and took out her phone. She'd waited a long as she could to call SAIC Lawson, not wanting to wake her supervisor up. It was currently a bit after 5:00, and she figured it was okay at this point. Hell, knowing Lawson, she may appreciate being roped into the case in such a way.

Lawson answered on the second ring and sounded very much awake. Even with a simple greeting so early in the morning, Lawson's voice carried the weight of command and an undercurrent of concern that was rarely doled out.

"Agent Flint…it's early. Is everything okay?"

"Not exactly."

As she and Jake got out of the car and started for their individual rooms, Tessa filled Lawson in as best she could. She ended it with the task she'd called in for—a task she knew would be difficult but might save a life.

"Lawson, we need eyes on Marissa Vale, ASAP," Tessa said, her tone brokering no argument. "She could be at risk, and we can't afford another blind spot."

"Do you know where she lives? Is she in your area?"

"We don't know for sure. I'm bringing it to you because I thought the bureau could get the information and provide the resources quicker than the local PD where we are."

"You're likely right about that. I'll make sure it gets done. And what about this other name? This journalist?"

"Lily Greene. I'm actively trying to get in touch with her. I've tired three times so far out there's no answer. Probably just not returning an unknown call at such an ungodly hour."

"Keep trying. And be sure to keep me posted. I feel like this one might be getting away from us."

But what Tessa heard was *I feel like this one might be getting away from you.*

"Will do," Tessa said, before ending the call with a firm click. The silence that followed seemed to press in on her, a stark contrast to the urgency that thrummed like a pulse beneath her skin – a condition she'd learned to monitor with clinical detachment due to her inability to perceive pain.

She and Jake had come to the sidewalk that ran along in front of the rooms. Jake's room was right next door to her, and he waved to her as he unlocked it.

"Get whatever sleep you can," he said. "I get the feeling this day is going to end up getting pretty crazy."

"Same to you," she said as she opened her door and stepped into the room.

Her eyes took in the bed and her body ached to collapse onto it. First, though, she had to try Lily Greene again just to try. She figured she'd leave another message and this time really push the urgency.

She dialed the number again—a Bangor number—and it went straight to voicemail. She figured Lily likely had a Do Not Disturb timer set on her phone. Her brows furrowed in frustration; time was a luxury they didn't have. She left a message that was terse and to the point, an urgent plea veiled in professionalism.

"Lila, this is Special Agent Tessa Flint. We've come across your name in connection with our investigation. It's imperative that you contact me as soon as you receive this message. Your insight could be critical." She paused, considering her next words carefully. "Please, stay safe and alert until we can speak."

With that, she disconnected and let herself fall heavily onto the bed, the bounce of the mattress accepting her weight without complaint.

The fabric of her jacket crinkled against the starchy hotel sheets as she lay sprawled, limbs splayed in an unconscious mimicry of surrender. She could not afford the luxury of vulnerability, yet here, in the solitude of Room 117, Tessa Flint—a woman who knew no physical pain—granted herself a momentary respite from the relentless pace of her mind. With her eyes shut, the world narrowed to the sound of her own breathing and the muted thrum of blood in her ears, a rhythm that mercifully lulled her into a shallow slumber.

In what seemed like mere moments, but was in fact a couple of hours later, the shrill ring of her phone cleaved through the silence of the room. It was a piercing call to arms that dragged Tessa from the depths of her nap. Sunlight filtered through the slats of the blinds, casting thin stripes across her face and the rumpled bedspread. That meant she'd gotten at least *some* sleep because dawn had been little more than a whisper on the horizon when she and Jake had arrived at the hotel.

Disoriented, she reached out with a practiced hand, her fingers closing her phone before bringing it to her ear.

"Flint," she answered, her voice gravelly from sleep but edged with the readiness of an agent always on alert.

The clock on the nightstand glowed a mocking green, digits forming the numbers 7:14 AM. She had managed to snatch only a fragment of rest—right around two hours. The lack of proper sleep was a familiar adversary, one that gnawed at the edges of her consciousness, but would not deter her resolve. She blinked rapidly, forcing clarity upon her senses, as she prepared to dive back into the case.

"Agent Flint?" an uncertain female voice said on the other line. "This is Lily Greene, returning your multiple calls."

Tessa's senses snapped to attention as Lily's voice filtered through the phone, each word crisp and tinged with an undercurrent of concern.

Without hesitation, Tessa swung her legs over the side of the bed, the coolness of the floor grounding her as she pushed off into action.

"Lily, thanks so much for returning the call. I can—"

"The messages sort of freaked me out. You think I might be in danger?"

"I'm not sure, though it *is* a possibility. If you'll give me a moment, I'm going to get my partner, Agent Sullivan so we can speak with you together. Is that okay?"

"Yeah, sure."

Beyond frazzled but quickly bringing herself awake, Tessa hurried out of the room. She didn't even bother slipping her shoes on, hurrying outside in bare feet. As she did so, she filled Lily Greene in on the details of the case and why she thought it was necessary to reach out to her. In going over it all, Tessa reached Jake's room and knocked loudly.

Jake answered within about ten seconds. She'd clearly woken him up and when he opened the door to reveal that he'd stripped down to just his boxer's Tessa cataloged the tempting sight of it in the back of her mind. Had they not been in the middle of a case with a potential resource on the phone, she may have found herself a bit flustered.

She mouthed *"Lily"* while pointing to the phone with her free hand.

Jake nodded and waved her in. As he went about sliding on a pair of gym shorts and a tee shirt, Tessa sat down on the edge of his bed and placed the call on speaker mode.

"Okay, Lily, you're on speaker mode with myself and Agent Sullivan."

"Okay…"

"So, as I said in my messages, we'd like to ask you a few questions."

Jake sat down next to her. They huddled around the phone, their two heads bowed like generals over a war table.

"First of all, based on what I just told you about the case and finding your name in a shady circumstance, we may have a police presence keep an eye on you. You're out of Bangor, correct?"

"Yes. And my name…I mean, if this guy was ripping articles out of magazines, it could just be a coincidence, you know? My name *is* on a lot of stuff concerning female winter sports."

"That could very well be the case. But the way things are going right now, I thought we should be safe rather than sorry."

"Okay. So…how do you think I can help?"

“We don’t know that you *can*,” Tessa said. “We were hoping that your up-close view of winter sports over the past year or so might provide us with some clues. For instance, can you think of any reports or incidents involving stalkers of winter sports victims that you're aware of?”

“Ah, jeez…I don’t think so. I mean, two years or so ago, there was the story with Alexandria Poulette, that Swedish snowboarder. She had a guy break into her home and try to abduct her. Turns out, he had this long-standing obsession with her. But as far as I know, he’s in prison. Also…er, that was in Sweden. So probably no help to you.”

“No, not really.”

“And it doesn’t need to be that big of a story,” Jake added. “Anything small or out of the ordinary help.”

Lily’s voice hesitated for a mere second before she spoke again. “Oh! You know what? Actually, yes. There was something odd a few months back during a snowboarding competition right here in Maine. Out on Sugarloaf, if I remember correctly. One of the girls you mentioned had been killed was there…Rachel Coolidge. But this didn't involve her."

“Still…what was it?” Tessa asked.

“There was this guy lurking around the athletes, taking an uncomfortable amount of interest."

"Did you report this?" Jake asked.

“Yeah, me and a few others, actually. So later, when this guy tried rushing one of the competitors, there was already security there, waiting.”

“Who did he rush?”

“I hate to say I don’t recall, actually. I *think* it was Ashley Mulder. A snowboarder. Young thing…like seventeen at the time. And you know…I took notes intending to follow up, but the story got shelved," Lily said, a hint of regret lacing her tone. "I can send what I have over to you."

"Thank you. That could be crucial," Tessa responded with gratitude, feeling a sliver of advancement in their seemingly endless pursuit. She paused, considering their next angle of inquiry, "One more thing—does a snowflake pendant mean anything to you? Perhaps some significance among the winter sports community? Maybe like an inside gag or something like that?"

"Snowflake pendant?" Lily mused. She took several seconds to consider this before saying, "No, nothing comes to mind. It's a common enough symbol in the industry, but nothing... *hidden*, as far as I know."

"Understood." Tessa's reply was terse, her disappointment fleeting yet palpable. She terminated the call with professional courtesy, feeling the weight of fatigue pressing down once more. Yet, beneath it, the kernel of new information fostered a cautious hope. They now had a lead, tenuous as it might be, threading its way through the murky depths of their case.

"Sorry," Lily said,. "I wish I could be of more help. This all sounds…well, it sounds awful."

"It truly is. And Mrs. Greene…I understand you have to uphold and respect your profession. But I would greatly appreciate it if you didn't go public with the entirety of this just yet. I know there's been lots of headlines and stirring about Elana Dean, the first victim, but the other two haven't quite cracked front-page status just yet. And I think when it does, the entire state might go into a bit of a panic.

"Yes, I understand. And I respected these young women far too much to exploit them. You don't have to worry about me."

"Thank you."

With a quick wrap-up and proper goodbyes, Tessa ended the call. She and Jake sat in silence for a moment, processing it all. Jake's room was similar to hers with its impersonal hotel decor and the faint smell of industrial cleaner that failed to completely mask the musty scent of overused upholstery. In these spaces, nothing ever felt entirely clean or comfortable.

"Alright," she said, more to herself than to Jake, "I guess we just have to hope her notes are helpful." Her eyes, however, did not move to the laptop where Lily's information would arrive. Instead, she looked to the window where the sun had grown brighter, starting another day.

She turned towards the door, every muscle in her body aching for rest, her mind a tumult of facts and faces.

"Tessa," Jake's voice stopped her mid-stride, a gentle timbre wrapped in concern. She pivoted to face him, noting the lines of fatigue etching his features, the way his hair stood in disheveled tufts, evidence of restless fingers running through it during their call.

"Are you okay? We're both running on fumes here. Not exactly the best state for a sharp mind." His eyes held hers, an unspoken understanding passing between them.

A ghost of a smile tugged at Tessa's lips. "I could say the same about you." There was a lightness to her tone, one that rarely surfaced, a thread of warmth weaving through the chill of their grim reality.

"Someone's got to watch out for you," he quipped back, thc corner of his mouth lifting in a half-smile that didn't quite reach his eyes, heavy with concern.

"Thanks, but remember, I can handle myself," she retorted, crossing her arms. Despite her exhaustion, a flicker of energy sparked at their banter. It was a dance of words they had grown accustomed to, steps memorized through countless hours spent in each other's company.

"Oh, I know. I think I might know better than most, actually." He chuckled, rubbing the back of his neck. "But hey, even the invincible Tessa Flint needs sleep."

"Invincible, huh?" She raised an eyebrow, the hint of a challenge in her gaze. There was something comforting about this familiar repartee, a momentary reprieve from the gravity of their work.

"Absolutely," he affirmed, his smile broadening, becoming real for the first time since the harrowing discovery at the cabin.

"Want to meet at the car in ten minutes?" she asked. "Maybe we can grab coffee and breakfast somewhere while we go over Lily's notes."

"Sounds perfect."

She hesitated before grabbing the knob and opening the door to return to her room. She allowed herself a deep breath, her thoughts lingering on Jake's easy smile, finding an odd sense of solace in the midst of chaos. They were partners in more ways than one, tethered by purpose and perhaps, eventually, something more.

And whatever unlabeled, unnamed things might exist between them, they only continued to grow with each day that passed hunting down killers together.

CHAPTER SEVENTEEN

Tessa's gaze was unyielding as she scanned the densely scribbled notes Lily had sent them. She and Jake had found a diner just five miles up the road from the hotel. Steaming mugs of coffee sat in front of each of them, and Jake's laptop sat in the center of the weathered tabletop. The gentle clinking of ceramic mugs and the soft hum of idle conversation blanketed them as a young, tired-looking waitress delivered their food. For Tessa, oatmeal and a single fried egg. For Jake, a western omelet.

Lily had sent photos of hand-scrawled drafts on notebook paper as well as three typed pages she'd started but never pushed beyond an initial draft.

"This is actually quite useful," Jake said, cutting off a piece of his omelet. "There's a clear-cut story in here for sure."

"And a strong lead."

Jake forked a clump of egg, ham, inions and whatever else was in the omelet into his mouth. As he chewed, he said: "So walk me through it. Tell us the story."

"And let my oatmeal go cold?" she asked in jest.

"It's oatmeal," he said with a shrug. "It's going to suck either way."

She rolled her eyes at him as she angled the laptop toward her so she could read the notes. She also had the digital files up on her phone.

"It looks like our next suspect is a man named James Meade. He tried to rush a downhill skier named Ashley Mulder after her event last winter." She felt a familiar twinge of urgency as she recited it all. This could be the lead they were grasping for in the murky waters of their investigation.

"Attempted to rush?" Jake echoed, his brow furrowed as he leaned closer. "As in, attack her?"

"Looks like it," Tessa confirmed, scrolling through the digital draft on her phone. "According to Lily's notes, there was a police report. And all it said was that Mr. Meade attempted to attack Mulder as she was coming off of the podium following an event. Security guards stopped him before he could reach her, but it apparently created quite the scene."

"This was at Sugarloaf Resort, right?" Jake asked.

"Yeah."

"That's not even forty-five minutes from here, So I wonder if Meade lives in the area."

Picking up her spoon, Tessa said, "Why don't you make that call and find out while I eat?"

He sneered at her playfully, and for a fleeting moment, Tessa wondered what it might be like to kiss him. She'd wondered this sort of thing before, but never right in the middle of a case. She shut the idea down right away, not wanting to get distracted.

With one last enormous bite of his breakfast, Jake relented. He made a call to the bureau to get a run-down on James Meade while Tessa began to eat her oatmeal—which *had* started to cool considerably.

As Jake spoke into the phone, Tessa's gaze wandered to the window. She watched the meager traffic roll by on the highway, heading into a day she hoped might finally bring her and Jake some answers.

***

Jake got all of the details for one James Meade of Severville, Maine by the time Tessa was finished eating. They came away with an address, a phone number, the fact that Mears was divorced, and the address of where he worked. Severville was an hour and fifteen minutes away from the doner—a distance that was almost far enough away for them to consider simply calling Meade.

In the end, though, both Tessa and Jake decided the safest and most through approach would be to confront Meade face-to-face. It was much easier to get a read on someone when they were standing right in front of you, unprepared for the questions coming their way.

"One hour and fifteen minutes," Jake said from behind the wheel after they'd started their journey to Severville. "Is that too much of a distance for a killer to be coming back and forth to this area?"

"I'm wondering the same thing," Tessa said. "It would certainly be possible, and a way to make sure he's nowhere near the crime scenes when the police arrive. On the other hand…you have to take into consideration where these women were killed. He knew their schedules. He knew where they were going to be. I think doing that sort of surveillance on someone would make that hour and fifteen-minute separation a real obstacle. But if there is envy at the heart of this—which I'm starting to think there is—I think they'd find a way."

It was a sour note that left them in mostly silence for the duration of the trip. As each agent remained lost in their thoughts, Tessa watched the wilderness and snowy regions fade away as Jake navigate to flatter expanses where two-lanes became highways and, little by little, businesses, fast food restaurants, and little strip malls started taking over.

James Meade's work address had him working at a rather large auto body shop, and his criminal record contained just the event at the ski competition and a charge of domestic abuse which, Tessa assumed, had led to his divorce.

Tessa was looking back over all of this information as Jake took an exit. The grey facade of the industrial park loomed ahead, signaling their arrival. The trip itself had gone by rather quickly, but she couldn't help but feel that the morning was getting away from them. And if that was the case, how much more a head start did their killer have on the next victim?

Jake parked in the large parking lot and the moment they stepped out of the car, the clang of metal on metal and the whirring of electric drills greeted them. The body shop was immense, nearly the size of a car dealership. They made their way into the central lobby which smelled of coffee and a very faint scent of grease.

There was a welcome desk with a large window looking into the repair wing of the building. Sparks flew like miniature fireworks as workers ground away at the skeletons of cars, transforming wrecks back into something resembling their former glory.

A perky, young blonde was sitting at the reception desk. She wore a button-down shirt with the company name on her left breast. "Can I help you?" she asked with a practiced smile.

"Yes, we need to speak with James Meade."

The girl nodded as she eyed them for a moment, apparently deciding it wasn't worth her time to ask questions. "Just one moment," she said. She grabbed the receiver from her desk phone and pressed a single button, switching on some sort of intercom back in the repair wing. Listening to the girl speak and also hearing the electronic murmur of her voice through the glass between the lobby and the repair wing made it sound as if the girl had a booming, authoritative voice.

"James, to the front desk, please!"

The girl put the phone down, still smiling. “You’re welcome to coffee or water while you wait,” she said, waving her hand to the right and gesturing to a small snack area.

“No thank you.” Tessa watched through the glass to see the response to the girl’s announcement. She took note of a man with a grease-stained jumpsuit glanced up from under the hood of a pickup truck, wiping his hands on a rag. He was stockier than his mug shot suggested, with a face weathered from long hours beneath harsh fluorescent lights.

He entered the lobby area through a door on the other side of the room. He looked to the desk, smiling at the receptionist, and then his eyes settled on Tess and Jake. Tessa wasted no time, walking right over to him.

“James Mead?” she asked.

“Yeah, that’s me. Can I help you?" His voice carried a guarded edge, eyes narrowing as they flickered between the two agents.

"We’re Special Agents Flint and Sullivan, FBI," Tessa stated, showing her badge. "We need to speak with you about an incident involving Ashley Mulder."

Meade’s expression tightened, a muscle ticking in his jaw. "Figures," he muttered, shaking his head. "Christ, I’m never going to live that down, am I?”

“Where can we talk?”

Meade thought about it for a moment, clearly irritated. “This way,” he said, nodding behind them to a thin hall that led deeper into the building. “We can use one of the conference rooms. Or we can do it right here for all I care. Trust me, it won’t take long.”

Tessa wasn't sure if this was said as an intended threat or just out of annoyance. He'd not been able to get a proper read on him yet to make such guesses.

“The conference room is fine,” Jake said.

They followed Dean across the lobby and down the hallway. He opened the first door on the left, revealing a small, generic conference room. The table sitting in the center of the space offered room for perhaps eight people. A single phone sat in the middle of it. Other than that, the room was pretty much featureless.

Meade plopped himself down into one of the chairs with a resigned sort of burden. Tessa sat as well while Jake opted to stand against the back wall, where a picture window looked out onto the parking lot.

"Mr. Meade, you've already discussed the incident with local authorities—" Tessa began, but he cut her off.

"Yeah, I told them everything. Twice." Meade leaned back in his chair, the irritation evident in his tone. "I don't know what else you want me to say. I sure as hell don't know why the FBI would get involved more than a year later."

"Indulge us," Jake interjected smoothly, always the diplomat. "We're trying to piece together a larger puzzle here, and your interaction with Ms. Mulder might be a key piece."

Well played, Tessa thought. *Lull him in smoothly without giving so much as a whisper to the idea that we're trying to figure out if he's a murderer.* Sometimes, she forgot just how keen and aware Jake could really be behind his forensics and logistical expertise.

"Fine," Meade sighed, crossing his arms. "But like I told the cops, it wasn't anything serious."

Tessa observed him carefully, noting the defensive posture, the way his eyes darted to the door as if contemplating an escape. There was more to this story; she could feel it in her bones. And while her own nerves never fired pain signals, her instincts were razor-sharp when it came to reading others' discomfort.

"Walk us through that day," she pressed, her gaze unyielding. "Every detail could be crucial."

Meade exhaled sharply, realizing these agents weren't going anywhere until he talked. He shifted in his seat, reluctantly unraveling the thread of his memory from that fateful encounter.

Meade's jaw tightened, a muscle quivering with contained frustration. He glanced down at his hands, calloused and stained with grease, before answering.

"My kid, she's a huge fan of Mulder. Been following her career for years," he started, his voice tinged with a mix of embarrassment and resentment. "She's only eleven years old…ten last year, and she wanted an autograph. She was waiting so patiently, so damned excited. But Mulder... she just walked right past her like she wasn't even there. And it wasn't like she didn't see us. She actually shook her head at my daughter and sort of rolled her eyes like she was too good."

"And?" Jake prompted, crossing his arms as he leaned against a filing cabinet, watching Meade closely.

Meade grimaced, as if the memory left a bitter taste in his mouth. "I had a few beers in me, more than I should've. There was this local brewery at the event, sponsoring it, I think. It got under my skin, seeing my daughter brushed off like that. So, after Mulder finished her event, I let her know what I thought. Rushed up to give her a piece of my mind after she'd gotten down off of that winner's platform."

"Is that all?" Tessa asked, sensing the story was incomplete.

"Look, I know it was stupid," Meade conceded, shaking his head. "But it wasn't about hurting anyone. I just... lost my cool for a moment, alright? I wanted to call her out in front of everyone…trying to stand up for my daughter in what I realized after the fact was the dumbest way possible."

Tessa believed him. Had there been any more to the story, the police file would have been more detailed. As it stood, he was detained, taken to a holding cell, and released just two hours later.

Tessa observed him in silence, her expression unreadable, then shifted gears. "Where have you been over the last week, Mr. Meade? Can anyone verify your whereabouts?"

For the first time, Meade's posture relaxed slightly, and he nodded. "Yeah. I haven't really gone anywhere. Working here mostly. Last night, I went out to catch a movie."

"Who were you with?" Jake inquired, his tone casual yet insistent.

"Janine, one of the painters here," Meade replied. "We saw that new thriller at the Cineplex downtown. You can ask her; we were together until late. Went out for a beer after the movie."

"When did you get home?" Tessa asked.

"Right around midnight. Maybe a bit earlier. I don't know for sure."

"And Janine works here?"

"Yeah. She's putting a decal out on a work truck right now."

Tessa nodded. She figured it wouldn't hurt to confirm the story with this Janine character, but based on Meade's authenticity and the easy availability of proving his alibi, Tessa already knew what they were going to find out. And if Meade's alibi stood, it would place him far from Emily Radley's murder scene, another dead end in a case riddled with them.

They'd hit another dead end.

"Thank you for your cooperation," Tessa said, standing up. She felt suddenly foolish for driving all the way out here, for eating almost three hours of what was already starting to feel like a pivotal day. Her mind was already racing ahead, calculating their next move. The truth was out there, shrouded in the shadows of doubt and deception, and Tessa felt the weight of the clock ticking ever louder. They needed to act fast before the killer struck again.

She was about to ask Meade to point them in the direction of Janine when her phone buzzed in her pocket. She quickly checked it, hoping it might be Garcia or Bowen or even Lawson with something new to help them along.

Instead, the caller display read ELLE.

She nearly let it go to voicemail; yes, she would love to speak with her friend and mentor, but Elle only ever called after hours, when she thought she stood less of a chance of interfering in a case. For her to call in the middle of the day…it might mean something. After all, Elle was the only other person aside from Jake who knew she planned to work toward opening up Sarah's case again.

"Agent Sullivan, would you mind confirming Mr. Meade's alibi with Janine?" Tessa asked. "I need to take this."

"Yeah, sure," Jake said, giving her a look that seemed to ask *Is everything okay?*

She nodded to him as she stepped out of the conference room. As she answered the call, she headed back toward the small waiting area in the lobby.

"Hey, Elle," Tessa answered, mustering a cheerfulness she didn't feel.

"Hey! Listen…I'm really sorry to call you in the middle of the day, but this is sort of pressing. Not super important or anything, but time-sensitive on my end."

"Okay. What's up?"

"I'm being sent to Portland for two days to follow up on a bank fraud case that started in DC. I leave today, and I know how you've always told me that if I'm ever in the neighborhood and need a place to stay…"

She left it unfinished, leaving it to Tessa to figure out. Tess was already smiling, excited about the prospect of spending some time with Elle.

"Yes. You're more than welcome to come stay at my house."

"How's that ocean water?"

"Cold. Also, listen…Jake and I are on a case right now, up in snow country and the resorts. In the chance I'm not back home by the time you get there, the key is—"

"Ah, don't tell me. Let me see if I can figure it out."

"Without breaking any windows, please."

"I promise nothing. Hey, thanks, Tess. I appreciate it."

"Of course! I'm looking forward to it."

"Same. Now…back to that case. Want to fill me in on the details?"

The truth of the matter was that she'd *love* to go over the case details with Elle. But she still felt that they were running out of time, feeling that they were working against the clock. Even now, having spent these three minutes speaking to Elle, Tessa felt that she'd wasted too much time.

"Not now. It's sort of a mess right now. Winter athletes and no clues. But maybe later, on my back deck with some wine."

"Sounds good. The wine and the deck. Not the winter athletes part. If you're up near Sunday River, there's a ton of them, from what I remember."

"Yeah, there are…" Tessa said, the passing comment striking her as important.

"Bye, Tessa. Stay sharp. See you soon."

As they ended the call, Tessa saw Jake approaching through the shop, seeing him through the glass. She thought about the random comment Elle had made and knew that it was time to finally pull the trigger on the one huge task she'd been dreading.

Jake came into the lobby shaking his head. "His alibi checks out. he also showed me the app for his credit card, backing up that he'd been at a bar watching a basketball game with friend on the night Rachel was killed. It's not him." He nodded to her phone, which she was bringing to her ear again.

"Who are you calling?"

Before she could answer, Lily Greene answered the other line. "Hello?"

"Lily, it's Agent Flint. I have another favor to ask."

"Sure. What is it?

" I need a list of all the winter athletes in the area," Tessa stated, her voice steady but insistent. "We have reason to believe they could be in danger."

"Are we talking your immediate area or all of Maine?"

"Let's start within a one-hundred-mile radius of Sunday River. Is that doable?"

"Yes. Give me about an hour."

"Perfect. Thanks. "

She turned to Jake, who had been silently observing her. "We warn them, we increase our visibility—make it harder for our perp to take another shot without exposing themselves."

"True," he said. "But it also alerts him…and it might drive him into hiding."

Tessa nodded, but her determination was unwavering. "Then I guess we'd better find the bastard before he gets that chance."

CHAPTER EIGHTEEN

The water sluiced over Tessa's body in a torrent of warmth, steam curling up around her like spirits eager to take away the day's weariness. She felt rushed in the midst of the relaxation, having stopped by the motel for a quick shower and a change of clothes—anything to get a recharged and re-focused feeling.

The sterile scent of motel soap filled the cramped bathroom as she scrubbed the grime of frustration and dead ends from her skin. She took no more than three minutes, making the aggravating decision to skip her hair altogether. Still, when she stepped out and toweled off, she did feel a bit more energetic. The mirror was fogged over, hiding her reflection as if protecting her from the disappointment of an unsolved case staring back at her. Tessa wrapped a rough towel around herself, relishing the abrasive texture against her skin—a sensation that reminded her she was still fighting, still feeling, despite the numbness that so often threatened to consume her.

Dressed in fresh clothes, she felt the beginnings of resolve knitting together inside her once more. As she brushed through her hair, there was a knock on the door—Jake, no doubt, ready to face whatever lay ahead. And as she walked over to open it, her phone rang again. This time, LAWSON appeared on the screen.

She took the call at the same moment she answered her door. It was, in fact, Jake. He'd also grabbed a quick shower; she noted that *he'd* had time to actually wash his hair and felt ridiculously envious.

"This is Flint," she said and then, looking at Jake, mouthed: *"Lawson."*

"Flint, it's Lawson," came the reply, her urgent crackling through the line with the urgency of breaking news. "I just wanted you to know that we've located Marissa Vale."

Tessa's hand tightened around the phone, the name sparking a trail of possibilities in her mind. "That's great. Where?"

"Bridgewater," Lawson said, the word heavy with implication. "Almost on the entire opposite side of the state from where you are. We assume that means she's safe from the killer, but she's still under watch."

A map unfurled in Tessa's mind, distances and jurisdictions stretching out like the tendrils of the investigation itself. Bridgewater was far, a whole new terrain of complications and bureaucracy that lay between them and Marissa Vale.

"Understood," Tessa replied, her brain already shifting gears, calculating routes and the time they would lose in transit. "You should also know that we've been speaking with Lily Greene, the journalist I told you about. She's supposed to be sending us a list of all female winter athletes in the area. It's now about twenty minutes beyond the time she said she'd get it to us, though."

"You expecting a big list?" Lawson asked.

"I simply don't know."

"Pass it along to me when you get it, and I'll get a team here at the office to help."

"Sounds good," Tessa said.

The call ended, leaving Tessa in the cramped space of the motel room, the air now thick not only with humidity but with the weight of expectation. She pocketed her phone and grabbed her badge, slipping it into her belt with a familiar sense of purpose. Jake watched her with a bit of weight to his gaze.

"So we get this list from Lily and then what?" Jake asked. "Just hope we get lucky?"

"A little luck never hurt anyone," she said as she clipped her holstered Glock to her side. "Especially with Lawson wanting to get so involved."

"That's not automatically a death sentence, you know."

She closed her eyes for a moment, trying to push away the images that surfaced unbidden: a young girl with bright eyes and a slightly crooked smile; her sister, gone without a trace, leaving a hole in their family that no amount of time could fill. Then, her mother's face, pale and still—another victim claimed by the ripples of that one disappearance.

"Hey," Jake's voice broke through her reverie, gentle yet firm. "You're doing that thing again."

"Sorry," Tessa said, opening her eyes. She didn't have to ask what 'thing' he meant. She'd been retreating more often into the past lately, especially when cases got tough.

"Maybe we finally talk to Gary now," Jake suggested. "Emily's boyfriend. We know he had a drug dealer, so I don't think it's outside the realm of possibilities that he may have links to other shady characters."

“I doubt he’s till at the precinct, though,” Tessa said. “Let’s get an address and have a talk with him.”

She was grateful to have the option ahead of them, but skepticism laced her words. They gathered their things quickly, a silent agreement between them that no time could be wasted.

***

The drive to Gary's place was a short one, but each mile seemed to stretch out before Tessa like taffy, as if teasing her as to just how long this day was going to be. The road was a blur of greenery and asphalt, bordered by a skim of snow on the edges, a monotone backdrop for her spiraling thoughts.

It all whirled into one single blur as Tessa once again allowed herself to dwell on Sarah. The thought of her sister had become the equivalent of a huge quest she could see but could not yet fathom starting. It was a mountain in front of her and she had no idea how to start climbing. She but she knew she had to. Even if the answers waiting at the top of that mountain were the ones she was dreading, at least she’d know.

But maybe the answers would surprise her. Maybe they’d even support the hope that she’d been clinging to all of these years, providing answers that would make the climb worth it.

"Have you been thinking about your sister again?" Jake asked, glancing at her from the driver's seat.

"Is it that obvious?"

"Only to someone who knows you well." His tone was compassionate but careful, like he was trying to navigate a minefield.

"Every unsolved case feels personal, but this..." She trailed off, unsure how to articulate the weight of her past colliding with the present. “Actually, this one *and* that last one with the pearl necklaces. Something about them just raise up a lot of unresolved crap from my past.”

"You know you can talk it all out with me, right?”

“I do,” Tessa said. “And *you* know that I have to process something to death before I really verbalize it, right?”

“Yes.”

“And that’s what makes us great partners,” she joked.

"Right," Tessa murmured, drawing strength from his conviction. She turned her gaze outside, where the landscape had shifted to the suburban sprawl that marked the outskirts of Gary's neighborhood.

They pulled up to a modest house, the front yard neatly trimmed. A sense of normalcy hung around the place, incongruous with the violence and mystery that had brought them here. It was the sort of house that got lost in its surroundings, a white-collar home among hundreds of others.

Jake parked along the curb, and before they could even make it to the thin and tidy porch, the front door swung open. On the other side, there was a woman with lines of worry etched into her face, wearing an apron dusted with flour. A younger man, presumably Gary, stood behind her. His eyes were red-rimmed, his posture slack as if the weight of the world pressed down on his shoulders. The scent of something sweet baking did little to mask the thick air of grief that enveloped the home.

"Are you the FBI agents?" the woman asked.

"Yes, ma'am," Jake said, showing his badge. "Agents Sullivan and Flint. We were hoping to have a word with Gary."

They'd come up to the porch now, and the woman did her best to smile at them. "I'm Janet, Gary's mother. Just trying to help him through this."

"That's understandable," Jake said.

Form behind his mother, Gary said, in a dry and broken voice, "Come on in."

Tessa stepped across the threshold, her senses attuned to the details of the house—not much int e way of decoration or furniture. It was clearly the home of a young man not accustomed to owning a home. It made her wonder how long he'd owned it and, based on what Bowen told them about Gary, how he managed to even afford it. Jake followed close behind, his presence a silent support she found herself relying on more than she cared to admit.

As they stepped deeper into the house, the sweet smell became more pronounced. Apples, cinnamon, and butter. Apple turnovers, maybe. Though it was Gary's house, it was his mother who led them through the hall, coming to rest in the kitchen. There, Tessa saw that her hunch was correct; a baking pan of turnovers had just come out of the oven, still steaming.

"They're Gary's favorite," Janet said. "You're welcome to have one if you'd like."

Tessa, sticking to her cardinal rule of always accepting food or drink from the grieving, smiled. "If Gary doesn't mind, I'd love one."

"Gary," Jake said, "we need to ask you some questions and some of them may seen harsh. We can do it here, or we can go somewhere in private."

"We're fine here," Gary said, looking sweetly to his mother. "I've told mom a lot over the past few hours. She…she…"

He stopped, making sure his emotions were in check.

"And if he wants me to leave the room, I will," Janet said.

She placed a plate with a fresh apple turnover in front of Tessa. The smell was intoxicating and had her mouth salivating at once. She then sat down at the end of the table beside Gary and reached out to take his hand. She gave it a squeeze and nodded to him as if telling him he could do this.

Tessa took a bite of the turnover and found it amazing. As she did so, her gaze met Gary's, noting the shadows beneath his eyes. "Gary, we're so sorry for your loss," she began, her tone devoid of the usual detachment she wore like armor. "But like Agent Sullivan said, we need to ask you some questions—anything that might help us understand what happened to Emily."

He nodded, swallowing hard. "I know. I want to help. The cops asked me so many questions…a few different ops, but all the same questions, So I know what you're going to ask. I just... I can't think of anything odd or upsetting. Em was happy. We were happy. I didn't always make the right choices, and we were…we were sort of risky with our behavior and all…but we were happy."

"Agent Sullivan and I came across Brent Fallen last night. He was near the scene where you found her…where you'd planned to meet. Does your mother know about Brent?"

Gary nodded, looking slightly ashamed.

"I'll tell you right now," Jake said, "that is alibi pretty much checks out. But do you think he may have it in him? To take a life?"

"No. He's the sort that talks a big game, but…no. I don't see Gary killing anyone."

"Sheriff Bowen tells us you'd left work at a diner and headed straight for the pond. Is that right?"

"Yeah. And one of the offices at the station already checked with everyone I listed off that I shared a shift with. There's at least five people who can confirm that I worked at the diner from four until closing."

Tessa figured this would be the case, given how passively Bowen had mentioned it. She tucked the nugget of information away and moved on.

“And did you hear Emily mention anything that really bothered her or scared her over the past few months?”.

“Nothing. I’ve tried so hard to think of *something*, but I swear…I really can’t think of a single thing.”

"Nothing at all? No changes in behavior or routine?" Jake pressed gently, his experience with the fragility of the human mind evident in the patience he exuded.

"Nothing," Gary insisted, his hands fidgeting in his lap. "She was training, focused on her competitions. That was Emily—always driven."

Tessa reached into her jacket pocket and pulled out her phone to show a picture of one of the pendants. As she did, she saw that somewhere in the course of their visit, Lily Greene had finally gotten in touch with them. Hopefully, with the list they'd been waiting on.

Ignoring it for the time being, Tessa showed Gary the picture.. "Have you ever seen this before?"

Gary's eyes locked onto the image, and recognition flashed across his features. As he studied it, Tessa continued to work on her turnover.

"Yes," he finally murmured, but there was some concern in his eyes. "It came in the mail for her. To her place in Rhode Island."

"Did she say anything about it?" Tessa probed, watching him intently.

"She thought it was from a fan," Gary replied, his voice distant as he recalled the memory. "Said it was flattering, but kind of strange. The package…it didn’t have a return address, and there was no note. Emily never wore it, though. She tucked it away in her jewelry box and never mentioned it again."

Tessa exchanged a glance with Jake, a silent conversation passing between them. This was a lead—a tenuous one, perhaps, but it was more than they had moments ago. A pendant sent through the mail, unasked for and ultimately discarded, yet somehow linked to Emily's life—and possibly her death.

“Just one last question,” Tessa asked. “Would you happen to know if Emily had any ties or connections to either Elana Dean or Rachel Coolidge?”

He thought about it for a moment, and Tessa could see the weariness in his eyes. She wasn’t sure how much longer he was going to be able to hold it together—before he had another meltdown moment.

“No, I don’t think so. I know who Rachel Coolidge is, though. Emily sort of followed her career. She was a big fan.”

Tessa wasn't sure if there was anything there to follow or not. But as she became more and more certain that Gary had nothing to do with the murder, she suddenly wanted to look at the text from Lily Greene.

"Thank you, Gary. This is helpful," Tessa said, her mind already racing with the implications. "We'll do everything we can to find out the truth."

"Please do," Janet said. "Emily was a sweet girl. And I think she turned Gary here around in more ways than he cares to admit."

As they rose to leave, Tessa felt the oppressive atmosphere of the house cling to her like a second skin. The normalcy of grief juxtaposed against the abnormality of murder left a bitter taste in her mouth that almost rivaled the apple turnover. She stepped out into the late morning sun, finding herself still slightly haunted by the loss and pain she'd seen in Gary's eyes.

Jake fell into step beside her as the exited the house, his presence a quiet reassurance. They didn't speak as they made their way to the car, the list from Lily an unspoken urgency between them. Tessa's mind raced as she pulled out her phone, eager to see what possibilities Lily's list would provide…if any at all.

CHAPTER NINETEEN

The car door closed with a definitive thud, sealing them inside their mobile think tank. As soon as Jake started the engine, Tessa opened up the text from Lily. As she'd hoped, there was an attachment to it. Lily's brief message read: *Sorry this took so long. Wanted to make sure I didn't leave anyone out!*

Tessa opened the attachment, and her heart seemed to lighten with relief. "Okay," she said. "it's not going to be as bad as we thought."

"How's that?" Jake asked, pulling away from the curb and pointing them back in the direction of the precinct.

"There are only fourteen names here. And Lily has even provided the hometowns of a few of them, which will make the searching much easier. She also has two of them marked down as *'currently injured and not competing'*."

Despite the relief she felt, there was still a gnawing tension coiled within her—the very same tension that had panted itself in her guts when they'd arrived at the private slopes where Rachel Coolidge had been killed. since the case began. She had imagined a labyrinthine web of athletes to sift through, a daunting task given their limited time frame. But this—fourteen was manageable. It was a number that whispered the sweet possibility of a breakthrough.

Jake glanced at her briefly, the lines around his eyes softening. "Good news then. We can divide and conquer. Maybe Bowen can offer a few warm bodies." His voice, typically resonant with confidence, now carried a note of fatigue.

"Exactly," Tessa replied, her gaze not leaving the paper. In every name, she sought an echo of the killer's motive, a shadow of intent. The car hummed beneath them, a steady thrum of power that mirrored Tessa's racing thoughts. There was an elegance to the way she processed information, an emotional detachment born from her inability to feel physical pain. Yet, she felt the weight of the case pressing upon her, the silent screams of injustice that demanded to be heard.

As they pulled into the parking lot of the station, the building loomed before them, its façade pockmarked by time and weather. It was small and unsuspecting much like the semi-rural community, but she knew that because of this case, the story inside was very different. She and Jake hurried inside, with Tessa remining herself that they now had fourteen names—fourteen lives they could potentially save. Fourteen names. Fourteen potential leads. Fourteen fragments of hope.

Inside, the precinct buzzed with the undercurrent of activity, a hive of law enforcement driven by duty and caffeine. Tessa's mind, always parsing details, noted the worn linoleum floors, the flickering fluorescent lights, the tired faces of cops too familiar with overtime. Everywhere, the scent of stale coffee and determination mingled, a signature perfume of the place. She'd noticed it all before, of course, during their first few visits to the building. But now that she felt progress was being made and that they could be angling in on the end of this case, she saw it all anew.

"Let's rally the troops," Jake said, a spark of energy igniting in his tone. "I'll see if Bowen is here."

Tessa nodded as she waved her way around a few desks, not quite sure where she and Jake were supposed to set up shop. However, as she moved quickly, her mind latched onto something…something she'd seen on the list in the car.

Jake, now several steps ahead of her, turned back as he sensed that she'd stopped walking. "Everything okay?" he asked.

"Fine," Tessa replied, her voice a controlled murmur, her mind still churning. "Just thinking about something…"

She wasn't ready to give voice to this budding theory—this idea in her mind that was barely even an idea at all just yet. Not until it was fully formed and defensible. There was something about the athletes Lily had marked down as injured, a piece of this macabre puzzle that beckoned her with a siren's call.

Jake nodded and turned to proceed deeper into the building. He'd take only two steps before a familiar voice called out to them from across what Tessa assumed was meant to serve as the bullpen—a collection of cluttered desks in the middle of a large room, situated behind a waist-high partition.

"Agents!" the voice called out.

Sheriff Bowen seemed even stockier while in the station. He hurried over to them and though it as clear he was trying to camouflage it, there was the merest glimpse of hope in his eyes.

"I hear you went out to Severville to speak to a suspect?"

"We did," Jake said. "Unfortunately, it was another dead end."

"But we do have something that may turn out to be huge," Tessa said. "And with your help, we may get some answers sooner than we were expecting."

"Okay. How can I help?"

Tessa showed him her phone, walking him through the details of how they'd gotten the list of female winter athletes from Lily Greene. The look of relief on his face as she explained it to him was, she supposed, the same she and Jake had worn when they realized there were only fourteen names to look into.

"So," Jake said, "we need a small team to help us run down these athletes."

"Text that to me, and I'll get some people together. This will be Priority Number One as far as I'm concerned." He then turned his attention to the bullpen area and the several officers milling around or sorting through papers and files at their desks. "Everyone listen up! Agents Flint and Sullivan need our help, and I need a few volunteers! Agent Flint, do you want to walk them through it?"

Tessa explained the situation again and within seconds, several officers and deputies assembled with an air of determination, their faces etched with the resolve that came from too many unsolved cases and sleepless nights. Sheriff Bowen swiftly delegated tasks, assigning each officer a trio of names from the list while emphasizing the discreet nature of the inquiries. They were to gather information, establish locations, and report back without alarming anyone unnecessarily.

But through it all, Tessa's mind kept going back to that one phrase on Lily's list.

Currently injured and not competing.

"Keep it tight, though," Tessa instructed, her tone leaving no room for error. "We don't know how close we are, and the last thing we want to do is spook the killer into hiding."

There were several nods and murmurs of acknowledgement as the team dispersed, each member embarking on their slice of the mission. With the sudden burst of motion and hope, Tessa felt the gears of progress grind into motion. This was what she lived for, the orchestration of efforts that would lead to a breakthrough. Every name checked could mean a step closer to the predator they hunted—a predator who had, until now, remained a ghostly figure, slipping through their fingers.

Jake leaned in close, lowering his voice. "You're onto something, aren't you? Outside of this list, I mean."

"Maybe," Tessa replied, locking eyes with him. Her intuition was seldom wrong, yet she knew the importance of evidence over hunches. "Give me another few minutes."

While Jake assisted Bowen with the logistics, Tessa found an open workspace and pulled up all of the case files they'd managed to collect so far. Emily Radley's death so was fresh that there wasn't much to go on in that regard.

She went back through every page, every note, searching. That, in tandem with the fragile framework of her new theory, had her hunting for even the smallest bit of evidence or circumstantial evidence they may have overlooked.

Tessa's fingers drummed a silent rhythm on the wooden edge of her desk, each tap a punctuation mark to the thoughts racing through her mind. The case files lay splayed before her, a mosaic of mugshots and incident reports that told a story but not the whole truth. Her eyes were drawn to the receipt for the bulk order of snowflake pendants—evidence that had led Bowen and Garcia down a false trail that had dead-ended.

The killer was clever. Dedicated. Driven by…by what? Hatred? Jealousy? Envy?

"Dammit," she muttered under her breath, leaning back in her chair. All around her, Bowen was assembling his team. A few officers had already filed into one of the conference rooms. She was still excited by the progress and felt they were on to something. But this one thing in her mind—this theory that was not yet a theory—was still getting in the way.

She pulled up a digital image of the payment transaction once more, scrutinizing the details. Whoever purchased these pendants had hidden their tracks well, too well for an amateur. The killer knew how to move unnoticed, how to predict the victims' locations with unnerving precision.

He planned this carefully, she thought. *This was more than just a whim, more than just someone moved by emotion. And with that much planning, there has to be something lurking behind it…a motive they may not even be aware of.*

As Tessa revisited the crime scenes mentally, retracing steps, timelines, and alibis, the notion of premeditation grew stronger within her. All the victims had been alone when they were struck down, vulnerable…while in a place they saw as comfortable.

She reached for Lily Greene's list again, her gaze settling on the annotations next to two names: "currently injured and not competing."

Her pulse quickened as she considered the implications, the isolation that an injury could impose on an athlete, the festering envy it could breed. Could the motive be rooted deeper than mere opportunity? Was the killer targeting what they could no longer have themselves?

Currently injured and not competing...careful planning...a lot of time put into this...

A chill ran down her spine, not from the sterile air of the precinct's records room, but from a realization crystallizing within her. That theory was now growing heavier, more than just a hunch now.

Envy, the silent whisper in the back of one's mind, could drive a person to unspeakable acts. It seemed that Tessa wasn't just chasing a ghost; she was after a shadow fueled by desire, by a need to extinguish the light in others that had dimmed in themselves.

The pieces of the puzzle were starting to form a clearer picture, guided by Tessa's relentless pursuit of the truth. Now, she just needed to find the connection, the missing piece that would lead her to the person behind the mask of the killer.

Without another thought, Tessa got out of her seat and walked across the room to where Jake was speaking with Bowen and another officer hunched over a laptop as they attempted to get the address of a name on the list.

"Agent Sullivan…a word, please?" she said.

He walked quickly over to her and move slightly away from the group so they could speak in semi-private. "You're going to tell me now, aren't you?"

"The names on Lily's list…the two that were injured. It has me thinking…what if that's our killer?"

"You mean one of the injured women?"

"No. What if it's someone who was sidelined, watching others succeed where they could not?"

Jake glanced at her, the creases around his eyes deepening. He'd seen enough pain, enough twisted motives in his career to recognize the seeds of truth in wild theories. "You think it's envy?" he asked, skepticism lacing his tone, but not dismissively so. He respected Tessa's instincts too much for that.

"Yes," Tessa affirmed, her gaze fixed on the rearview mirror as if the answers might be trailing them in the night. "Envy can fester, turn malignant over time. We've both seen it happen. And an injured athlete…if they're injured in a way that robs their future from them…all they have is time. Time to stew, to plan."

"Could be a longshot," Jake conceded, but he was already looking toward the door, ready to make a move on this hunch. "But you've got a point. We need more than what we have."

"Exactly. I want to build another list. A list of local winter athletes who've been injured in the past several years. But not just ones competing at a professional level. I'm talking everyone in the area…"

"Even kids falling and breaking bones on the ice?"

"Okay, so maybe not everyone. But you understand what I'm saying, right? Anyone would may have injured themselves that…I don't know…might have been *hoping* to make it to a highly-regarded or professional level."

"That could take some time. You thinking Lily again?"

"No. We'll find the local newspaper. If there was an injury of that magnitude—something that was brutal enough to cause someone to become this killer—it would be newsworthy."

"You're thinking news archives?"

"Yes. A mid-sized area like this, they'd keep records of everything sports-related. Game reports, injuries..."

"Alright," Jake agreed, smiling in that way she was starting to find both cute and a bit disarming. "Let's dig up the past, then."

CHAPTER TWENTY

The offices for the News and Herald, just three blocks away from the police station, was as quiet as a tomb. As Tessa and Jake entered, the only noise was the whispered clicking of someone typing in a hidden room. As they walked inside, Tessa was a bit surprised by how small the building was. A reception desk sat in s mall lobby, with one person stationed behind a large desktop monitor.

A young man of about twenty or so sat at the desk—an intern, Tessa assumed. He was dressed rather professionally, but it was apparent that he was not used to wearing such clothes. He looked unnecessarily uncomfortable, as if his entire body itched but he could not scratch it. He had brown hair that was little more than a mop of curls and the sort of trendy glasses Tessa had always associated with Buddy Holly.

"Excuse me," Tessa said, approaching the desk. "We need access to the archives. Urgently."

The young man opened his mouth to respond was cut off when both Tessa and Jake showed their badges.

"Oh! Feds…okay! Yeah…I can show you where it is."

A quirky smile played on the young man's lips as he stood, his lanky frame unfolding like an accordion. "Follow me, I'll take you to the treasure trove. Name's Dylan, by the way." His cheeky demeanor contrasted the gravity of their task, but Tessa couldn't fault him for not understanding the shadows they chased.

Jake gave her a quick nod, the silent communication between them honed by years of partnership. They had no time to waste on pleasantries; every tick of the clock was a reminder of the sinister thread weaving through the town's history.

Descending a narrow staircase that spiraled into the building's heart, Tessa felt the temperature drop, the air growing cooler and stiller. The sub-floor was dimly lit, lending an almost secretive aura to the place. Here, nestled between stone walls and under dust motes dancing in the shafts of light, were three laptops, their screens glowing softly.

"These beauties are your gateway to the past," Dylan said, his voice hushed in reverence to the silent chronicles that surrounded them.

"Everything's been digitized back to '75. Anything older than that, and you're going to have to dig through cabinets upon cabinets in our annex."

"I don't think we'll need anything that old," Jake said.

"Sweet. Well, it's pretty simple. Just type in your keywords and let the hunt begin. If you've got dates, names and locations already at your disposal, it's super quick."

Dylan demonstrated the search function with a few taps and swipes, his fingers flying over the keys with practiced ease. The database responded instantly, promising a wealth of information at their fingertips. Tessa noted the intuitive software, designed to pierce through decades of data.

"Let me know if you need anything else," Dylan offered, before turning to climb the stairs. That smile was still on his face. Tessa figured this was the most exciting thing he' experienced all week.

She settled in front of one laptop, her gaze fixed on the search bar. It was a portal to another time, one that might hold the key to unraveling the identity of their killer. She started to type, the click-clack of keys accompanying her thoughts. She had a vague idea of what she was looking for, and hoped the database would clue her in to the rest.

She started with simple searches, things like *winter sports injury* and *winter sport accidents.* Her eyes flitted across the screen as articles and headlines cascaded down in an endless torrent of information. She was diving into an ocean of past events, searching for the one drop of detail that could break their case wide open. The soft hum of the laptop's cooling fan accompanied her journey through digital back issues, a stark contrast to the tense silence that enveloped the subterranean room.

It took only five minutes before she realized that she was going to have to narrow the search down Maybe searching by individual sports would help.

"Anything yet?" Jake's voice cut through, tinged with impatience from the monitor beside her.

"Still looking," she replied, without glancing his way. Tessa knew Jake's disposition well enough by now; he thrived on action and immediate results, whereas she found solace in methodical research. This was probably not other boring him, but starting to irritate him as well.

Jake sighed heavily, shifting in his seat. "I just feel like we should be out there, pounding the pavement, not sitting here scrolling through old news."

"Every piece of this puzzle matters, Jake. We just need to find the right one."

He grunted in acknowledgment but said no more. His eyes returned to his own screen, clicking with visible irritation from page to page. Despite their differences, Tessa felt a thread of respect for her partner's eagerness to contribute, to be part of the tangible chase.

Turning her attention back to the task at hand, Tessa refined her search parameters. She entered terms like 'skating accident,' 'winter sports injury,' and snowboarding accident.' The list narrowed, and she began to comb through the incidents—a litany of mishaps and tragedies, each one a story frozen in time. The click of the mouse was rhythmic, almost hypnotic, as she delved into accounts of broken bones and shattered hopes.

"Look at this," she murmured under her breath, leaning closer to the screen. An article about a skier who had suffered a concussion was particularly detailed, highlighting the risks athletes faced. It felt close, but it wasn't what they were looking for. Tessa could sense the mounting pressure, the tick of the clock in her own head reminding her that every second they spent here was a second the real perpetrator roamed free.

"Concussions... ski lift malfunctions... frostbite..." She read aloud, a trace of doubt seeping into her voice. "It's all here, but none of it seems relevant."

"Are we barking up the wrong tree?" Jake asked, mirroring her thoughts. He ran a hand over his face, the lines etched there speaking to years of chasing demons, both within and without. “Maybe we’re getting too desperate. Maybe we’re looking for things that just aren’t there.”

"I'm starting to think you might be right," Tessa admitted. She hadn't reached her position by being stubborn; flexibility was key in their line of work.

"Let's give it a few more minutes." Jake's tone softened, perhaps sensing her concession. It was a dance they had become accustomed to—one leading, then following, as the rhythm of the investigation dictated their steps.

Tessa agreed with a nod, refocusing. Yet, as her fingers hovered above the keyboard, ready to abandon the digital maze, she worried that she'd made a mistake. First, shed' felt that the visit to James Meade had essentially been a waste of time, and now this. And time wasn't something they had in abundance. She drew in a breath, preparing to voice her surrender, to suggest they join the tangible pursuit with Bowen and his men beyond these walls.

But as she turned to Jake, her gaze caught the sudden shift in his posture. His shoulders squared, eyes narrowing with the precision of a hawk sighting its prey. The irritable energy that had surrounded him seemed to evaporate, replaced by an intense focus that anchored him firmly to the chair.

"Wait," he said, his voice a low command that halted her words before they could form. "Look at this. Damn, Tess...*look at this.*"

Tessa leaned in, her own sense of urgency reigniting as she peered over his shoulder. On the screen was an article, the date stamp indicating it was from four years prior. It detailed a high school hockey game — an event that would have faded into obscurity amongst countless others if not for the tragedy it described.

A promising senior player, the star of his team, had suffered a catastrophic injury during the final moments of the season. The article painted a picture of a young man—Hutch Pearson—with a future in professional hockey, a dream cultivated since childhood and about to be realized through college scholarships. But in one swift, brutal play, his knee was practically demolished, tearing apart ligaments and aspirations alike.

Tessa felt a pang of sympathy for Hutch Pearson. She imagined the agony of shattered dreams, the kind of torment that didn't show on X-rays or leave scars that doctors could stitch up. It was a familiar narrative, one that resonated within the depths of her being, where empathy and understanding intertwined despite her condition.

"Jake," Tessa whispered, her voice tinged with the weight of revelation, "this could be it. This... this is more than just an injury. This was life altering. If nothing else, I think it's wort at least seeing if this guy lives around here."

They exchanged a look, a silent conversation that required no words after years of partnership. The significance of their find was unmistakable, the implications far-reaching and chilling. Where there had been doubt, now there was a lead — solid, undeniable, and demanding further investigation.

The air around them seemed to thrum with possibility, the kind that only came in the moment of a breakthrough. Tessa's mind raced ahead, plotting their next move, already reaching for her phone to call Bowen with the name that might unravel the mystery entwining them all.

Tessa looked to the article, paying attention to the two pictures included with it one was Hutch's senior yearbook photo. He was smiling, surely looking ahead to a future where he was going to be able to make a living by playing the sport he loved. He was a good-looking kid with shaggy brown hair and a big, wide smile.

The other picture told a story of its own, though. The image, black and white yet stark against the dull glow of the laptop screen, showed a scene that was all too visceral despite its frozen state. A young athlete, grimacing in pain, was being hoisted off the ice by his coaches. His eyes were squeezed shut, a mask of agony etched onto his youthful face. But it wasn't the pain that captured Tessa's attention; it was the glint of metal against the player's chest.

"Jake…do you see that? In the picture?"

The look on his face was all the answer she needed. His eyes had gone slightly wide, and he'd all but gotten up out of his chair.

In the picture, Hutch Pearson was wearing a necklace—a snowflake pendant, identical to the one linked to their case.

The air between them crackled with tension, the kind that heralded a storm brewing on the horizon. Jake leaned closer, his breath quickening as he squinted at the pendant. His brow furrowed, recognition dawning in his eyes. For a moment, there was silence, punctuated only by the soft hum of the computer and the distant, muffled sounds from the library above.

"Damn," he exhaled, the word hanging in the space between them like a verdict. "That's our link. Three victims, one pendant, and now him."

The room suddenly felt smaller, more intimate, as if it harbored secrets it was reluctant to part with. The scent of musty paper mingled with the electric undercurrent of discovery, creating a cocktail of anticipation and dread.

Without another word, Tessa reached for her phone, the device suddenly heavy with the weight of implication. She placed a call to Bowen, her pulse thrumming in her ears as she waited for the sheriff to pick up, the seconds stretching into an eternity.

"Chief Bowen," she said when the line connected, her voice steady despite the adrenaline coursing through her veins. "We've got something. A lead from the archives. We need an address for a Hutch Pearson. And we need it *fast.*"

The room around her blurred, the edges softened, but Tessa's focus remained razor-sharp. They had a name, a symbol, and a trail to follow.

The hunt was on.

CHAPTER TWENTY ONE

From the shadowed alcove where the Zamboni usually rested, he watched her graceful pirouettes and aggressive sprints across the ice, an isolated figure of determination. The rink was practically deserted, save for a middle-aged couple holding hands on the other side of the rink, their laughter echoing hollowly in the expansive space. But it was not them he observed with such intensity; it was Courtney, the next symbol of all that had been ripped away from him.

His fingers toyed with the edge of his jacket, the fabric whispering secrets only he could hear. Like the three who had come before her, he knew Courtney's routine by heart now: the way she would slash at imaginary opponents with her stick, the steady cadence of her skates carving into the chilled surface, each motion a taunt to his damaged knee. How effortlessly she played, oblivious to the dream she lived—one that should have been his.

The rink's artificial chill seeped into his bones, a reminder of the countless hours he'd spent in similar arenas, where the scent of cold metal and the sharp tang of ice had once signified hope. Now, they were just accomplices to his twisted sense of justice. His eyes remained fixated on Courtney as she halted her practice, panting, beads of perspiration glistening like diamonds on her forehead—an athlete in her prime, unaware of the fate that loomed so close.

She glided towards the bench, hand brushing her hair back as she reached for her water bottle. It was then that she saw it—the snowflake pendant deliberately placed beside her gear.

He almost smiled when her confident stance wavered. He could imagine her heart rate spiking with alarm. She understood its significance. The symbolic calling card left with Rachel Coolidge and Elana Dean before their light was extinguished. Surely she'd seen the news articles, maybe seen it on the local news.

He relished the moment, savored her dawning terror like a fine wine. The pendant—its intricate design mimicking the unique beauty of frozen fractals—was more than a mere trinket. It was his declaration, a chilling promise of what was to come. He'd had one not too long ago, before his life had been taken from him by one careless stumble from an opposing player.

And now he was gifting it to them…to those he was claiming.

As Courtney's gaze flitted nervously around the rink, searching for the threat she sensed but couldn't see, he pressed further into the darkness, moving toward the locker rooms and away from the glaring lights over the ice.

The pendant had done its job—the seed of terror planted firmly within her mind. Maybe she feared she was next. Maybe she thought someone was just playing a sick joke on her.

He watched her shiver, not from the cold, but from the ice forming around her heart. It was delicious, this moment before the chase, the electric tension of predator and prey trapped in a frozen dance. He imagined her thoughts racing, trying to piece together the puzzle of survival, unaware that he had already predicted her every move. That's what made it so satisfying—the knowledge that no matter how fast she skated, she could never glide past the shadow of death.

In the frozen expanse between them, destiny advanced with stealthy grace. And as Courtney's instincts surely told her something was amiss, he prepared to strike. He knew it was risky here, in mid-day. Hell, maybe she'd take that pendant to someone at the front desk and report it. He certainly hoped not, but the mere idea that it might somehow enhance his hunt was a bit seductive.

He watched closely, almost admiringly, as Courtney walked to a nearby trashcan along the edge of the rink grounds and the check-in and equipment areas on the front of the building. With a flick of disgust, she discarded the pendant. Ah, but it had served its purpose, a psychological trap sprung with precision. Besides, he had another in his pocket—the one that would go around her cold, dead neck.

He watched as she then went to her phone, perhaps texting a friend or her parents. Maybe she was telling them about the pendant, about how scared she was.

Whatever she was saying, it would be the last thing she put out into the universe. And something about that made him suddenly beyond anxious to take her, to slip that necklace around her neck as he looked into her dead eyes.

With calculated patience, he remained shrouded in the shadows, allowing her the illusion of control. Let her think she was fine. Let her believe for one more heartbeat that survival was within grasp. For when the time came for him to step into the light and close the distance between them, he would relish the look of recognition—the dawning of understanding when Courtney realized that the rink was not her sanctuary, but her tomb.

The air in the rink was still, charged with the tension of a predator's patience. He stood perhaps thirty feet away from here and now, here she came. She was headed for the locker rooms, as he knew she would. She clutched her hockey stick like a lifeline, the cold of the metal seeping into her palms, offering a false sense of security against the lurking threat.

He watched, unseen, his eyes tracking her every step until he had to hide away in the locker room. He knew no one else was there, as he'd checked it just five minutes before. Besides…he'd be done shortly…as would she.

Already, he imagined that he could taste the sharp tang of her fear, a flavor he found more intoxicating than victory on the ice ever was. His envy of her, of all they represented, coursed through him like an icy surge. They, who glided effortlessly where he had fallen. They, who soared where he had been grounded.

His knee ached with the memory of betrayal, the moment when bone and sinew gave way under the strain of a dream too heavy to bear. It was a constant reminder of what was taken from him—what he now took from others in a twisted reclamation of his destiny.

Slowly, barely able to contain himself, he slunk back into one of the showers. He pulled the curtain taught to hide himself and then waited for the sound of the door to open…for the sound of Courtney Satterfield walking directly toward her death.

CHAPTER TWENTY TWO

Tessa never saw Jake more engaged and focused than when he was driving to a destination with a sense of urgency behind him. While Tessa was quite the driver as well, she knew that Jake had a bit of a gift for maneuvering just about any vehicle at high speeds though busy streets. And that was what he was doing in that very moment, navigating the narrow streets that led to their destination. Tessa's hands were clasped tightly in her lap, knuckles whitened from the grip. Every second seemed to stretch, her mind racing with the possibilities of what they might find at the residence of Hutch Pearson.

She looked down to her hand, wondering if he was squeezing them too tightly. If she cracked her knuckles or even broke her fingers, it wasn't like she would know. All she knew was that there was a lot of pressure down there, and her knuckles had gone white...so she loosened up a bit.

"Almost there," Jake said, his voice steady despite the urgency that propelled them forward. He knew this because Tessa had plugged the address Bowen had given the into her GPS, and her phone was sitting on the center console between then.

The car swerved into a suburban neighborhood, houses lined up like domestic dominoes. Jake slowed a bit and then, as if he'd been driving along perfectly normal for the past ten minutes, pulled up into the shallow driveway of a generic-looking home, its drab exterior belying the turmoil that likely churned within its walls.

"Let's go," she said, her voice low but threaded with anticipation. Without waiting for a response, she stepped out of the vehicle, her keen gaze scanning the perimeter. No movement, no signs of life—just an eerie stillness that settled over the place like a shroud.

Jake followed suit, fishing out his lock-picking kit as he moved. As he worked on the front door, Tessa found herself analyzing him—the methodical way he manipulated the tools, his unwavering focus—a mirror image of the diligence he applied to every case. It was one of the many moments he realized just how safe she felt with him and how perfectly they suited one another.

The soft click of the tumblers falling into place signaled the next step. Jake nudged the door open with his shoulder, and they stepped over the threshold into the shadowed interior. The air was heavy with the weight of unspoken stories, each room a potential hotspot of evidence. Their footsteps were muffled by the carpet as they moved in tandem, alert to any sign of the killer they were so close to apprehending.

In the dim light filtering through the curtains, Tessa's pulse quickened. This was it—the lair of a murderer, the endgame of their chase. She could almost taste the victory, bitter as it was, knowing that it came hand-in-hand with the tragedies carved by the killer's hand. She pushed the thought away; empathy was a luxury she couldn't afford in moments like these.

Jake gave her a brief nod, a silent signal between two partners who had learned to communicate beyond words. Tessa stepped into the living room, her movements slow and deliberate. The carpet beneath her feet was immaculate, each fiber combed to uniformity, betraying no hint of the sinister. Yet the air was stagnant, a stillness that seemed to cling to the faded wallpaper and well-kept furniture like an invisible residue. She inhaled deeply, trying to detect the scent of fear or violence, but found only the mustiness of disuse.

"Feels like no one's really lived here," she murmured, more to herself than to Jake. Her gaze swept over the room, searching for anything out of place—a sign, a clue, something that would scream 'guilty.'

"Or someone's gone to great lengths to make it seem that way," Jake replied from behind her, his voice low and cautious.

Tessa nodded, her lack of response not due to disagreement but rather deep contemplation. She remembered the abandoned cabin they had scoured earlier in their investigation; its dust and decay were in stark contrast to this almost obsessive neatness. A thought struck her, cold and sharp as a blade. "What if this is where our cabin-dweller came from?"

Without waiting for Jake's reply, Tessa moved on, her senses heightened, scanning every inch of space for something amiss. Her condition, the inability to feel pain, had always forced her to rely on other senses, to be acutely aware of her surroundings. It was both a curse and a blessing in her line of work, and now she harnessed it with full force.

They found themselves in the kitchen, a tableau of normalcy with a magnet holding up grocery lists on the refrigerator door and a few dirty dishes in the sink. But it was the stack of mail on the counter that caught Tessa's eye. She sifted through the envelopes, each bearing the name they had been chasing— Hutch Pearson. It was a tangible connection, an X that very much marked the spot.

"Got something?" Jake asked, stepping up beside her as he watched her face, looking for the telltale signs of discovery she couldn't hide.

"Confirmation," Tessa said, holding up the envelopes for him to see. "This is the right place." She felt a surge of triumph, quickly smothered by the weight of responsibility. Knowing they were in the killer's home added gravity to their search—each room held potential answers, each drawer could unravel the mystery further.

"Let's keep moving," she said, her voice steady. "Every second counts."

As they continued their search, Tessa's mind whirred with possibilities, analyzing each detail, preparing for the moment they would piece together the final evidence they needed to end the chase. But the house remained stubbornly silent, withholding its secrets until they unearthed them from the shadows.

Along the main hallway—a stubby little space that contained only a single bathroom and a bedroom—a nondescript door opened up onto a set of stairs leading down into darkness. She stepped into the bedroom first, slightly shocked by what was waiting for her.

The walls were plastered with Boston Bruins memorabilia, a shrine to hockey greatness that felt oddly out of place in this suburban home. A hockey stick, its handle worn from years of grip and play, hung on the wall like a relic. Tessa's eyes swept the room, noting the way such items mingled with personal effects—a juxtaposition of public fanaticism and private life. As for the bed, it was neatly made, and everything else was just as tidy.

"Ugh, the Bruins," Jake whispered humorously from behind her—just trying to break the tension.

They walked back out into the hallway and faced the door that presented a set of basement stairs. "Another basement," Tessa sighed. She looked back to Jake, tilted her head toward the stairs, and walked through the doorway.

As she descended the creaking basement stairs, her hand grazed the cool wall for balance. The musty scent from below filled her nostrils. Not a smell of disuse, but one of dust being stirred up—the smell of stifled movements. At the foot of the steps, she paused, allowing her eyes to adjust to the dimness, her ears tuning in to the silence that seemed to cloak each corner.

As Jake came to the bottom of the stairs behind her, the basement sprawled before them, a cavern of shadows and boxed-up memories. In the far corner, she spotted a sliver of light emanating from beneath a door. With Jake at her heels, Tessa approached, every sense alert. She gripped the doorknob, turned it with a faint click, and pushed the door open to reveal an office space that reeked of obsession.

It was a small, right space packed with a single desk, a small and weathered table, and a chair. Just enough room to be considered a workspace. And it did look like work had been done here—dark and devious work. A laptop sat on the desk, the lid closed. In the scope of the room, it seemed unnaturally dangerous.

"Look at this," Jake murmured, drawing her attention to the cluttered desk. Magazines were strewn across it haphazardly, their pages dog-eared and marked with sticky notes. Tessa leafed through one, her fingers brushing over an article about a local figure skater—a beacon of potential tragically snuffed out.

And many of the faces looked familiar.

"That's Elana," Jake said from behind her, pointing.

"And this one is Emily," Tessa said, pointing to a glossy picture of Emily Radley posing in front of a large cluster of fir trees.

"There's more here," Jake said, his voice tight as he gestured to the pictures pinned methodically across the opposite wall. Tessa's gaze followed, studying each photograph. The faces of the girls looked back at her, their smiles frozen in time, unaware of the cruel fate that awaited them. Her chest tightened—not from fear, but from a resolve hardened by too many cases, too many faces.

Then her eyes landed on a photo set apart from the others. A high school senior, mid-play on the ice. His face was angled toward the camera without knowing the picture was being taken. The action of a game-in-progress was presented in blurry shapes behind him.

She'd seen this same kid in the same outfit before. It was Hutch Pearson—likely in the same seasons before he'd blown out his knee. The snowflake pendant couldn't be seen in this picture, but she assumed it was tucked away beneath the pads and underlayers.

"Got him," Jake said firmly from beside her.

Tessa opened the laptop and wasn't at all shocked to find that it was password protected. The glow of the screen cast her face in sharp relief as she cycled through potential passwords, each attempt met with a stubborn denial. She retraced her steps mentally, piecing together the obsession with a team that was more than fandom—it was an identity.

Maybe there was something to be found in all of the Bruins memorabilia.

"Try 'BobbyOrrFour,'" Jake suggested, his voice low but edged with the urgency of their mission.

She did, and got nothing. "Any other guesses?"

"Eh, not really a hockey guy." He took out his phone and started running some searches on his browser. Tessa knew it was necessary but felt like they were wasting time. After about thirty seconds, Jake said, "Okay, how about 'Neely…Nelly something, Neelyfan'? Try that."

She put this in, aware that this would be the fourth attempt and at some point, the system would lock her out. The password didn't work. "No good," she said.

"Okay…um, how about Neely2005."

She typed this in, worried that it would be wrong and lock them out. But really, what other choice did they have? They had to at least *try*.

She typed it in…and it turned out Jake was right, though. The computer presented them with the desktop home screen. "Good job. How did you know?"

"I typed in *famous Bruins players* and Cam Neely came up more than anyone else. He was inducted into the hall of fame in 2005."

With the laptop unlocked, Tessa saw that Pearson's internet browser was opened, but minimized.

She clicked on the icon, and the page expanded, revealing a figure skater caught mid-pirouette, her form a study of grace under pressure. It was a video that had been paused, showing Courtney Satterfield—another name to add to their grim list. She was easily identified by the title of the video.

Hopefully, there was already police protection in place for Courtney, but there was no way to be sure just yet…not without losing themselves in a string of phone calls.

"Check the search history," Jake prompted, peering over her shoulder.

With a few deliberate clicks, Tessa pulled up the search history. It was mostly videos. And there they were—Rachel Coolidge, Elana Dean, Emily Radley—each girl's name a terrible echo of the past, their routines observed by unseen eyes. The pattern was undeniable, a sequence of interest that culminated in this latest object of fixation.

Tessa felt no shiver, no goosebumps—her body denied her those warnings—but her mind bristled with heightened alertness. She knew that somewhere out there, a clock was ticking down, measuring the moments until another star was extinguished.

Tessa's fingers flew over the keys, her mind working at a feverish pace as she connected the dots that sprawled across the digital landscape. Courtney Satterfield, poised and elegant on the ice, unaware that she was the subject of such malignant scrutiny. The room seemed to close in around Tessa as she internalized the urgency of the moment, the walls whispering secrets of a killer who had blended into the shadows of everyday life.

"Jake, we have to move—now," Tessa said, her voice cutting through the dense tension like a blade. She rose from the desk, leaving the ghostly glow of the laptop screen behind. Jake nodded, his jaw set in grim determination, understanding the weight of what lay before them.

CHAPTER TWENTY THREE

"Where to, Tessa?"

Jake's voice was an anchor, keeping her afloat as they got into the car. It was an important question, but more importantly, it was one without an immediate answer.

"Give me a sec," she replied, not even glancing his way. The cool detachment in her voice wasn't new to him. Jake knew Tessa's history, how her inability to feel pain had shaped her into the relentless force she was today. Her focus was her strength, and right now, they needed it more than ever.

"Do we have the contact info of the women from Lily Greene's list?"

"Some…the locals. They were thrown together back at the precinct first thing."

"Do you have any of them on you?"

"Yeah, like I said…the locals."

"Good. Call Courtney Satterfield. Place it on speaker. You mind if I drive?"

He grinned and shook his head. "Not at all."

Tessa understood that in the heat of a case, she could come off as being bossy and controlling. Jake knew these things about her but rather that find them irritating, he seemed to enjoy it. Hell, sometimes it was almost as if he fed off of it. He got out of the car without argument, already scrolling to find Courtney's number.

By the time he was in the passenger seat and Tessa had taken the wheel, he'd found the number and was typing it in. He set it to speaker and though the call connected without a problem, the ringing seemed to stretch on forever, a suspenseful symphony amidst the silence of the car.

Jake glanced at Tessa, watching as her jaw tightened when the voicemail greeted them instead of a live voice. A bright, happy voice told them that she was unable to come to the phone.

Tessa bit back a curse. Every second mattered, and this felt like a setback. But setbacks had never deterred her much. If anything, they propelled her.

"Any chance you can get the number of her parents?"

"Sure," Jake said. "I can reach out to Bowen again. Damn…he's going to get tired of hearing from us."

"Not if we end up catching this bastard."

Tessa still wasn't quite sure where they needed to go, but she hated the idea of sitting still. So she pulled the car away from the curb as Jake called Bowen. She headed in the direction of the precinct because now that it seemed they were in something of a holding pattern, it seemed the most intuitive decision.

"Bowen, we need Courtney's parents' numbers, please," Jake said. "Uh huh…yes, that's fine." He then looked to Tessa and said: "I'm on hold…"

More wasted time, she thought. It was infuriating to know who the killer was and who he was going after—information they didn't have just an hour and a half ago—and not being able to instantly act on it. But just seconds later, Jake was reciting a number being read to him by Bowen from the other line.

"Thanks, Sheriff," Jake said. He ended the call and instantly inputted the number into his phone. He again set it to speaker, placing the phone on the center console.

The phone began to ring and as the second and third buzzes chimed through the car, Tessa could literally feel the tension; it was as if there was a ghost hitching a ride with them in the back seat.

Pick up, pick up," Tessa murmured, a rare hint of desperation threading her usually steadfast tone.

The phone rang a fourth time, and then there was a click and a skeptical-sounding voice.

"Hello?" It was a woman…Courtney's mother. And though Tessa's heart went out to her, she wasted no time.

"Mrs. Satterfield, this is Special Agent Flint, with the FBI. I have no time to fill you in on specific details right now, but I need to know where Courtney might be right now."

There was a brief pause, a mother's hesitation shadowed by fear. "She... wait, the FBI?"

"Yes, and we—"

"Is Courtney in some sort of trouble?"

The truth came out before Tessa could stop it. But she needed to express the urgency in a way that got the point across. "Yes, we think she is. My partner and I desperately need to find her."

"I…oh, she's…" It was clear the mother was scared, confused, and maybe even skeptical. But in the end, the love and concern for her daughter won out. “She should be at the Corner Rink. She trains there every Friday without fail."

“That’s an ice-skating rink, I assume.”

“Yes, and—”

"Thank you." Tessa ended the call abruptly, her gaze locking onto Jake's profile as he kept his eyes on the road. "The Corner Rink," she said, the name tasting like a lead on her tongue. "That's where we'll find her."

Understanding flashed in Jake's eyes, and he nodded, his hands tightening on the steering wheel. He punched the location into the GPS, and the device chimed with confirmation. Eight miles out. They had a direction, a tangible thread in the web they were untangling.

“Christ…let me call the mother back,” he said. “She deserves to know.”

Tessa nodded, knowing he was right. Jake re-dialed the number and began speaking on calming, soothing tones to the mother. But in that moment, Tessa barely heard any of it. All she could think about was getting to the Croner Rink…and hoping they weren’t already too late.

As they sped down the highway, Tessa's mind raced through the possibilities of what they’d find. She knew how these killers operated; they thrived on control, on the meticulous planning of their crimes. But this afternoon, Tessa and Jake were the unknown variables, the disruptors. And Tessa relished the thought of breaking Hutch Pearson's pattern before he could claim Courtney Satterfield as his next victim.

***

Tessa was beyond subtleties and stealth when she pulled the car into the Corner Rink parking lot. She didn’t waste time with an actual parking spot, choosing instead to bring the car directly to the entrance, pulling up alongside the curb.

The building itself looked more like an arcade center than a skating rink. From the outside, it almost resembled a bowling alley. Tessa scanned the establishment, a small-time haven that seemed to cling to a bygone era. The arcade's neon signs buzzed faintly in the encroaching twilight, casting a lurid glow over the cracked pavement. At the back, a bar window flickered with the light of a television, likely broadcasting some sports game to an audience of locals nursing their drinks. It was both strange and a little charming to think that an ice rink was somewhere inside.

Tessa stepped out of the car and hurried inside, Jake falling in beside her. The front doors led opened onto a lobby boasting hardwood floors. There was a greeter's podium at the back edge of the foyer, but it was currently empty. Beside this was a small sign that gave directions via arrows as to where everything was located. The Corner Rink offered not just a skating rink, but a bar, an arcade, a lounge area, and gift shop. Without any hesitation at all, Tessa and Jake headed to the right and down a dimly lit, carpeted hall—the direction of the skating rink. And the closer they got to it, the colder the air became.

When they finally saw the ice, Tessa understood the layout and allure of it a bit better. The rink itself was positioned to the back of the building, an area of about fifty yards by fifty yards. The ice was surrounded by protective fencing, decorated to look unassuming and soft.

However, there was no sign of Courtney. In fact, Friday afternoons at 2:15 were apparently not an ideal time for skating sessions; the only people on the ice were a middle-aged couple gliding uncertainly with smiles on their faces.

"Maybe we missed her?" Jake suggested.

"Keep looking," Tessa replied, her gaze locked on the rink. There was a narrative written upon the ice, one of frantic energy and desperation. The surface was marred by skate marks, fresh and jagged, cutting through the frozen layer like panicked brush strokes on canvas. They were too erratic, too forceful to belong to the couple who now rested on the sidelines, hands entwined and cheeks flushed from exertion.

No, these were the marks of someone with practiced speed and precision. These were the imprints of haste, of quick turns and sudden stops. Someone had been pushing their limits here.

"Look at the ice," she said, pointing it out to Jake. "Those marks are recent. And skilled."

Tessa took a very fast lap around the rink, moving by the row of lockers where personal items and secrets could be stowed away. With each step, she prepared herself for what they might find, the pieces of this deadly puzzle they were so determined to solve. The chill of the rink seeped through her jacket, but it couldn't touch the resolve that burned within her.

Tessa's gaze swept across the rink. The scent of chilled metal and old leather permeated the air, spartan benches lining the walls. Her instincts hummed—a harmony of anticipation and dread—as she strode toward the far back corner of the rink. Here, the benches and lockers came to an end and opened up for a slightly darker space that led to the locker rooms. Each step resonated on the linoleum, a staccato march that seemed to beat in time with her quickening pulse.

The locker rooms, she thought. *Maybe she's changing out of her workout clothes...*

As Tessa headed in that direction, a scream splintered the stillness. It was muffled and brief, but it was present enough to cut through the layers of her resolve. For a split second, that sound seared into her memory, an auditory brand marking this moment as one of pivotal gravity. She halted, every nerve ending alert, her lack of physical pain heightening her focus rather than dulling it.

"Jake!" she hissed, adrenaline flooding her system.

Jake hurried closer, leaving his place over by the lockers where he's been investigating something. His right hand was hovering instinctively over his holstered Glock.. They exchanged a glance that conveyed volumes; years of partnership had honed their communication to near-telepathy. Tessa's hand found the butt of her gun, the familiar weight a grim reassurance.

"Maybe in the locker rooms," Tessa said. And speaking it out loud seemed to inject some urgency into it. If Courtney *had* gone into the locker rooms and the place was this slow at this time of the fay, it would be a perfect place for their killer to strike.

They hurried forward, propelling themselves with trained urgency toward the source of the scream. The corridor blurred past them, a tunnel narrowing to a single point around them. Within Tessa, the clinical detachment she often experienced in moments of crisis crystallized into laser-sharp concentration.

The door loomed before them, a barrier to be breached. Tessa felt it may be a bit of an over-reaction, but she drew her Glock. She wasn't going to take any chances. Her fingers tightened around her firearm, her thumb flicking off the safety with a click almost lost in the rush of blood in her ears.

"Ready?" she breathed.

Jake nodded, though he did seem slightly taken aback that she'd drawn her weapon.

Tessa pushed the door open with the force of inevitability, their guns leading the way as they swept into the room.

CHAPTER TWENTY FOUR

The chill of the ice rink had seeped into the very walls of the locker room, causing each breath Tessa took to form small clouds in front of her face. The place smelled of sweat and metal, a tangy scent that reminded her of blood. The fluorescent lights above buzzed like a horde of lazy flies, casting a sterile glow over the rows of lockers. As they approached, the scream they heard earlier echoed in their minds, a piercing reminder of the urgency at hand.

Jake, with his seasoned instincts honed from years on the field, nudged ahead of Tessa, his gun steady in his hands. His eyes scanned the room methodically, cutting through the shadows for any sign of movement. Tessa followed close behind, her own weapon gripped tightly as she mirrored Jake's vigilance. Their footsteps were muffled against the rubberized flooring, the silence almost suffocating.

It was a silence that was a bit unnerving and disarming. And perhaps that's why there was a moment when both Tessa and Jae froze when the figure suddenly appeared from behind a row of lockers. The figure had pivoted from the right, roughly ten feet away from them as he lunged forward, brandishing a hockey stick like a medieval weapon. Its arc was swift and precise, targeting Jake with a vicious intent. There was no time for warning shouts or evasive maneuvers. The stick connected with a sickening thud against Jake's head, sending him crumbling to the floor in an instant. Blood trickled down his temple immediately, his eyes glazed over by the force of the blow.

"Jake!" Tessa's cry was instinctive, a sharp contrast to the tomb-like quiet of the room. Her attention snapped to the assailant, registering the killer's wild eyes and the heaving of his chest. She leveled her Glock at him, but she had only a heartbeat to take it in before the hockey stick was swinging toward her.

Tessa's reflexes, untamed by her inability to feel pain, kicked in. With a dancer's grace, she twisted her body to the side. The hockey stick grazed her arm instead of striking her head. The impact was still fierce—a blow that would have stunned anyone else but merely caused Tessa to lose her grip on her gun. It clattered to the ground, skidding across the floor and coming to rest under a bench.

There was no pain from her arm, just a ghostlike tingle that came in waves—a distant sensation she knew should hurt but didn't register beyond the mere knowledge of it. She locked eyes with the killer, knowing the next move could be deadly. Her mind raced, calculating her options while Jake groaned on the floor, trying to shake off the effects of the hit. A drop of blood fell from his head to the floor, setting the stakes for what was to come.

Tessa's body was a coiled spring as she launched herself at the killer, her training taking over where her senses were dulled. She hit the assailant with the full force of her momentum, and they tumbled to the ground in a chaotic whirl of limbs and desperation. The air whooshed out of her lungs as they hit the cold, hard tile of the locker room floor. In the scramble, her eyes caught sight of Courtney Satterfield, sprawled awkwardly near a row of lockers, her chest rising and falling with shallow breaths.

"Stay down," Tessa breathed out, not knowing if Courtney could hear her over the sound of her own struggles. A pang of something akin to empathy shot through Tessa for the injured girl, but she shoved it aside. There was no room for distraction now, not when every second counted.

The killer—a man she now assumed to be Hutch Pearson—writhed beneath her, his face a mask of panic and rage. Tessa fought to keep him pinned, her hands grappling for any advantage. But he was strong, wildly so, fueled by fear or madness. And for a moment, Tessa feared she might be overpowered. Each time she thought she'd secured a hold, he bucked and twisted, throwing her off balance. On one such occasion, she would have been thrown off if her left shoulder had not solidly connected with the lockers beside them.

Then, the killer's arm swung around, aiming a vicious blow at Tessa's head. Instinct told her this would be a debilitating strike, one to knock her senses loose and leave her vulnerable. But the blow landed, and... nothing. No pain bloomed across her skull, no stars burst in her vision. She blinked, stunned only by the brief sense of vertigo.

He didn't know—couldn't know—about the quirk of her biology that made her impervious to the pain that would have crippled anyone else in that moment. Her head snapped back into position, eyes fixed on the killer with a renewed ferocity.

His confusion was palpable—a brief flicker of doubt that she seized upon. With the precision of a collegiate wrestler, Tessa leveraged her weight and flipped him onto his stomach, pinning him down with an iron grip. His jaw smacked against the floor as he thrashed beneath her, but she was relentless.

Tessa's muscles drew tight, every sense honed on the man beneath her. His breaths came in ragged gasps, his body a writhing mass of desperation trying to escape her grasp. He was stronger than she was—that was evident right way—and he managed to reverse the position. He quickly rolled her onto her back and instantly began to choke her His hands were like vices around her neck; she wasn't sure she'd never felt such pressure at her neck…but only pressure; there was, of course, no pain for Tessa.

Which could be deadly She had no idea how much more pressure would be required to snap her neck, her pain receptors lacked that sort of radar. For all she knew, she could be just seconds from death. She had to figure a way out of this, and…

His knee…

Her thoughts went back to the news archives, the bit about his injury. The injury that had sidelined him for good.

With a calculated shift of her weight, she stopped struggling and drew her leg up as far as she could—which wasn't as far as she would have liked, given her position on the floor. Still, leaning only slightly, she was able to bring her leg up just enough, positioning it where she hoped it might do the most damage.

In what felt like an odd sort of yoga, she bent and twisted her leg at an angle just behind his back. She then drove her heel into the side of his kneecap with surgical precision. The reaction was instantaneous—a sharp, guttural cry tore from his lips as his body went limp, his fight extinguished by the flare of pain Tessa could only imagine.

She didn't pause to relish the scream or the sudden ease with which she was able to shove him off of her. Instead, the moment he hit the floor, she pinned her knee into his lower back, drawing his arms behind him. Panting, Tessa snapped the cold metal cuffs onto his wrists, the click echoing through the locker room like a gavel declaring the end of a long trial.

"Pearson, you are under arrest," she announced, her voice low but carrying an edge that sliced through the tension.

From the corner of her eye, she saw Jake stir, pushing himself up from the ground with a groan. Blood trickled down the side of his face from a wound hidden within his hair. But his eyes, those sharp detective's eyes, were alert as they met hers, a silent message of relief and respect passing between them.

"Good work, Tessa," he managed, his voice rough with pain. His eyes still look cloudy, likely an indication of a concussion.

Tessa merely nodded, her focus shifting as she surveyed the aftermath of their confrontation. The locker room was a chaos of scattered equipment and echoes of the struggle that had just ended. And there, only feet from where Pearson now lay defeated, Courtney Satterfield remained sitting on the floor with her back against the wall, her breathing shallow but steady.

Tessa allowed herself a single moment of vulnerability, a brief exhale where the enormity of what could have been lost settled over her like a heavy cloak. But it was the glint of something silver on the floor that caught her attention next—a snowflake pendant, intricate and delicate, meant as a macabre gift for the young skater they had come too close to losing.

"Looks like you won't be needing this anymore," Tessa murmured, crouching down to pick up the pendant. Her fingers brushed against the cold metal, the irony not lost on her that such a beautiful object had been intended as a token of such ugliness.

"Courtney, are you okay?" she asked.

Courtney nodded. "He…He…was trying to strangle me when he heard you coming in. He…"

"It's okay now, Courtney. We're going to get you some help."

"Jake," she called softly, "Are you going to be okay? What do you need?"

"Nothing right now. Let's just get her some help."

He was already reaching for his phone, his eyes still hazy. But all the same, he dialed in the call for an ambulance and a few patrol cars to help with the clean-up.

As Jake was on the phone, Tessa stood sentinel over the captured killer, the snowflake pendant clenched in her fist. This was victory, bittersweet and hard-won, and though she couldn't feel the physical pains that marked the battle, the weight of the responsibility and the lives touched by violence hung heavy in her heart.

Yes, she'd saved Courtney Satterfield, but what about the others?

She tucked their images away deep within her heart where they would haunt her a bit forever. And with Sarah's image there as well, they were in good company.

CHAPTER TWENTY FIVE

The chill of the evening air couldn't compare to the cold that seemed to emanate from Hutch Pearson as he was led away in handcuffs. Tessa's gaze followed Bowen and the deputy as they secured the killer into the back of a patrol car, his presence an unwelcome stain on the snow-dusted asphalt outside the Corner Rink. She hovered close to Courtney, whose arms were wrapped tightly around her torso as if she could hold herself together that way.

"Good riddance," Jake muttered under his breath, his tone laced with a lingering grogginess from the blow to his head. Despite her inability to feel pain, Tessa understood the toll it took on him; the fight had been brutal. She admired his resilience silently—Jake never complained, facing his discomfort with a stoic grace that both baffled and impressed her.

Courtney shivered, and Tessa's attention snapped back to the girl. The young athlete's eyes were wide, reflecting the fluorescent lights that buzzed overhead. They flickered momentarily, casting long shadows across the group and adding a touch of eerie disquiet to the scene. Tessa placed a reassuring hand on Courtney's shoulder, trying to offer some warmth, some semblance of safety now that the threat was neutralized. But the girl's tremors spoke of terror that wouldn't fade with the mere application of handcuffs. She was probably only four or five years younger than Tessa, but in that moment she was much closer to a scared the-year-old child.

"Is he...?" Courtney couldn't finish the question, but she didn't need to. Her gaze was fixated on the departing police car, the red and blue lights painting her face in surreal hues.

"He's not going to hurt anyone else," Tessa assured her, her voice firm despite the chaos that had unfolded just moments before.

Before more could be said, a car pulled up into the Corner Rink parking lot, speeding with such recklessness that Tessa thought it was going to plow into one of the police cruisers parked in front of the building. A woman burst from the driver's seat, her face etched with lines of worry and relief all at once.

“Mom…” Courtney whispered as the woman came running in their direction.

Courtney was able to take only a few steps forward before her mother was there, wrapping her in an embrace that spoke volumes. Tears mingled with laughter, a release of pent-up fear and the joy of a reunion that had almost been stolen by tragedy. The father also came out of the car and hurried over to join in, his face solemn but relieved.

"Thank you," the woman breathed out, her words directed at Tessa and Jake as she clung to her daughter. "Thank you both so much."

Tessa felt a rare swell of emotion, something beyond the void where physical pain should have been. This was why she endured the hospital visits, the isolation—the chance to make a difference, to pull people back from the brink. She nodded, accepting the gratitude with a solemn sense of duty fulfilled.

"Of course," Tessa replied, her voice steady even as the weight of the day's events began to settle upon her shoulders. Jake, standing beside her, offered a warm smile that reached his eyes, a silent echo of Tessa's sentiments.

They watched for a moment longer as Courtney and her mother remained locked in their embrace, two figures finding solace in each other after a harrowing ordeal. It was a small beacon of hope amidst the darkness—a reminder that, sometimes, the monsters didn't win.

Tessa guided Jake away from the tender scene, her hand gently pressing against his back. The frigid air nipped at them as they made their way across the parking lot. It wasn’t quite three in the afternoon, but none of that mattered. After two and a half days of the chase, time no longer matters. She was tired and ready to call it a day. She could appreciate the victory later.

"Let's check that head of yours," Tessa murmured, concern lacing her words even though her expression remained stoic.

"Ah, it's nothing," Jake protested with a dismissive wave, but Tessa could see the slight grimace he tried to hide. His usual warmth was clouded by pain, and she knew better than to take his bravado at face value.

"Sit," she ordered as they reached their car, her tone leaving no room for argument. She popped the trunk, rummaging through their gear until her fingers closed around the first aid kit.

Jake obeyed, perching on the edge of the trunk. Tessa studied the cut along his brow. It was a jagged line, angry and red against his pale skin. It was nasty, but she didn't think it was going to be deep enough to require stitches.

Tessa peeled open a disinfectant wipe, the sharp scent cutting through the afternoon air. Gently, she dabbed at the wound, cleaning away the traces of blood.

"Does it hurt?" she asked, despite knowing he'd downplay any discomfort.

"Just a scratch," Jake replied with a tight-lipped smile. But there was a tension in his jaw that betrayed the impact of the blow he'd taken earlier.

For a moment, as she leaned closer to inspect the laceration, their faces were inches apart. Tessa could feel Jake's breath, warm against her cold cheek. There was something unsaid hanging between them, a palpable tension that had nothing to do with the s harrowing events in the locker room. Slowly and with great care to her touch, she used a bandage to cover the cut, her fingers resting on the side of his face a bit longer than was necessary.

"Thanks, Tessa," Jake said softly, his voice breaking the silence. His gaze held hers, gratitude mingling with something deeper, more vulnerable.

"Partners look out for each other," she stated matter-of-factly, pulling back slightly to create some distance. There was a brief flicker of disappointment in his eyes before he masked it with a nod of agreement.

"Yes, I suppose they do," Jake said. "But let's not make a habit of this," he joked, sliding off the trunk, his equilibrium restored now that he was patched up. He stood by her side, a testament to their shared strength. Together, they had weathered another storm—one that had brought them closer, even if neither was ready to acknowledge it just yet.

"There's going to be paperwork," Tessa said, watching Bowen's car pull away with Pearson in the back.

"But I don't want to do paperwork right now," Jake argued, mimicking a child. "We can do it in Portland. I'm beat, Tessa."

"Yeah, me too."

"Then let's call it Tessa." Jake's voice was weary from the ordeal as he opened the passenger side door and settled into the passenger seat. "We can head back to the hotel, crash, and worry with the clean-up in a few hours. Back at home."

He leaned his head back, closing his eyes for a moment, the darkening bruise along his temple a stark reminder of their narrow escape.

Tessa nodded and took her spot behind the steering wheel. As she reached for the ignition, her hand stilled. *Elle.* Her mind sharpened at the thought. "Can't do that, Jake," she said, her tone decisive. "Elle's passing through tonight. I promised I'd be there."

"Oh, that's…nice," Jake murmured, opening one eye to glance at her. A smile teased the corner of his lips. "She'll enjoy hearing about this ordeal, huh?"

"The case or specifically the part where you got whacked with a hockey stick?"

"Both."

"Okay, fine. Are you good to drive? Because I'm not."

"Yeah, I'm fine. You need to see a doctor. You may have a concussion."

"We'll see."

Tessa started the engine and started to maneuver her way through the remaining law enforcement vehicles on the scene. As they exited the Corner Rink lot, Tessa felt the finality of the case settling around them like dust after a storm. Hutch Pearson, the man who had taken the lives of three promising female athletes, was now securely locked away in the back of a patrol car, his reign of fear abruptly ended.

Jake remained silent beside her, the rhythm of his breathing steady and even. His resilience was something she secretly admired, even if she couldn't quite relate to the pain he must have been feeling. Her own lack of physical sensation was both a blessing and a curse—a barrier that often made her feel disconnected from experiences others took for granted.

She focused on the road ahead, the familiar hum of the engine a comforting constant in the aftermath of uncertainty. The killer was caught; Courtney was safe. And for now, that was enough.

As she headed back toward Portland—a nearly two-hour drive ahead of her—the silence between her and Jake felt like the calm after a storm; it was an absence of noise, but not of thought or emotion. She could feel Jake's gaze periodically on her when he wasn't dozing, assessing, perhaps reflecting on everything they had been through.

"Hey, Tessa," Jake said at some point roughly midway through the drive. "I never really said it before, but I guess I should."

"Said what?"

"I've never let you know how much I trust you. With my life, actually. There aren't many people I can say that about."

His words hung in the air, weighty and sincere. Tessa's hands tightened momentarily on the wheel before she relaxed her grip again.

She knew trust wasn't something Jake offered lightly, nor was vulnerability, and hearing it from him now meant more than he probably realized.

"Jake," she began, glancing his way while keeping her eyes mostly on the road, "trust goes both ways. You've got a knack for reading people, getting into their heads. But with you, what you see is what you get. And that's rare." She paused, considering her next words carefully. "I might not feel pain, but I feel other things. Loyalty, gratitude... trust. I trust you, too."

He nodded, a small smile touching the corners of his mouth, somehow making him look even more tired.

As the car sped towards home, the tension that had wound so tightly around them began to unravel. They were partners, yes, but in this moment, they recognized each other as something more: confidants in a world where certainty was a luxury and trust was a very rare thing indeed.

CHAPTER TWENTY SIX

The evening sky was a deepening shade of violet as Tessa navigated her car down the winding coastal road leading to her house. The rhythmic sound of the waves crashing against the rocky shore below mingled with the murmur of her car engine, offering a semblance of calm after the day's madness. She had just dropped Jake off at his own place with his insistence that he was okay and would go to the ER tomorrow if he still felt woozy.

Tessa pulled into her driveway, the gravel crunching under the tires like a brittle lullaby. As she killed the engine, the silence of the early evening enveloped her. She saw no other cars in her driveway, so she assumed Elle hadn't yet arrived.

As Tessa got out of her car, happy to be home, her phone buzzed insistently in her pocket. SAIC Lawson's number flashed on the screen. With a sigh, Tessa answered, briefing the Special Agent in Charge on the case details with concise precision. Lawson's voice, a blend of sternness and concealed concern, acknowledged the information before ending the call with a rare note of warmth directed at Tessa's relentless dedication.

Once inside, Tessa's home greeted her with its familiar embrace—the scent of salty air mixed with the subtle fragrances of home: laundry detergent, dish soap, and the reheated burger she'd had for dinner three nights ago. She shed her coat, her movements mechanical, and made her way to the small study that doubled as her sanctuary and workspace. The glow from her laptop screen flickered to life as she sat down, brushing back strands of hair that had managed to escape her usually impeccable bun.

Tessa began to type, her fingers tracing the keys with an urgency driven by the need to document every detail while it was still seared in her memory. She felt the need to get the details down now, while it was still fresh, hoping to make light work of the case notes tomorrow. But exhaustion was a persistent foe, creeping along the edges of her consciousness, tugging at her eyelids, and weighing down her hands. Her vision blurred, her normally stoic and focused demeanor succumbing to the physical toll of the past days' events. The words on the screen danced and merged, becoming indecipherable smudges of black against white.

With each passing second, Tessa's resolve crumbled. Reluctantly, she pushed the laptop away, the clatter of the keys falling silent. Her head slumped forward, chin nearly touching her chest, as she admitted defeat to the weariness clawing at her body—a rare moment of vulnerability for someone who had spent a lifetime mastering control over her painless existence.

Tonight, the case notes would have to wait. Tessa needed rest, and the comfort of her couch offered a temporary haven from the pressures of her job and the haunting memories that too often accompanied her solitude.

Tessa's consciousness teetered on the edge of oblivion, nestled within the embrace of her own living room. The couch beneath her was neither plush nor unyielding; it was familiar, supportive in a way that only years of use could contour to one's form. Her mind, usually a fortress of disciplined thought and analysis, now drifted away from the world of the living. It was a welcomed descent into darkness that promised a brief respite from the relentless pursuit of justice.

She dozed in and out, restlessly, until there was a knock at the front door. The knock was gentle yet insistent, a sound incongruously alien in the soft cocoon of Tessa's nap. It nudged her awake, beckoning her back to awareness with a persistence that could not be ignored. With great effort, her eyelids fluttered open, rebelling against the seductive pull of sleep. She groaned softly as she peeled herself off the couch.

Tessa shuffled to the door, her feet dragging across the cool hardwood floor, grounding her with each step. She fixed a mask of alertness onto her features as she twisted the doorknob, steeling herself for the professional facade she was accustomed to presenting. But when the door swung inward, revealing Elle's warm, welcoming smile, the pretense melted away.

"Elle," Tessa said cheerfully, relief and affection mingling in her tone. They embraced, an easy gesture between old friends, before stepping apart.

"Look at you, all worn out," Elle observed, concern etching her brows as she took in Tessa's pallor and the fatigue shadowing her eyes.

"Long case," Tessa murmured, brushing off the concern with a half-hearted smile. "And no, I don't want to talk about it."

"Never a dull moment," Elle quipped as Tessa ushered her inside. "Hey, I brought dinner!" She held up a plastic bag as evidence. "Thai!

And after that, you should get some real rest, Tessa. Forgive me for saying so, but you look like pureed crap."

"Thanks," Tessa conceded, feeling the weight of the past days pressing down upon her once more. "But what kind of host would I be if I go to bed right after you arrive?"

"A lazy one."

The snickered at this as Tessa walked through the house and to the sliding glass doors in the living room. She opened them and they stepped outside, feeling the cool sea breeze. The sun was inching closer to the horizon, casting a golden hue over the roiling waves, and for a moment, Tessa forgot the exhaustion clawing at her bones. The back porch was her escape, a place where the relentless push of the tide mirrored the constancy she sought in life.

"Wow," Elle breathed out, taking in the vast expanse of water stretching before them. "This is incredible, Tessa. Makes me want to move out here."

"It's pricey. Well, not for me. I inherited the house. Sort of."

"Oh, yeah. How did that go again?"

Tessa smiled wanly and said, "Yeah, I don't want to talk about that, either." She looked out to the ocean and looking at it lovingly. "I don't come out here as often as I should." She pulled out two chairs, motioning for Elle to take a seat as she went about uncorking a bottle of wine.

The clink of glasses punctuated the stillness that fell between them, a comfortable silence born from years of shared experiences. Tessa took a sip, the rich red liquid a sharp contrast to the saline tang of the sea air. Elle had brought Thai food—pad Thai and green curry, their go-to comfort food from academy days—and the aromatic spices mingled with the briny scent of the ocean.

"Here's to old friends and new beginnings," Elle toasted, raising her glass towards Tessa. A faint smile tugged at the corners of Tessa's lips, and she clinked her glass against Elle's before taking another sip.

"New beginnings," Tessa echoed, though her thoughts were far from fresh starts. They ate in silence for a while, the only sounds the rhythmic lapping of the waves against the shore and the occasional cry of a distant seagull. As the sky turned to deep shades of purple and pink, the day's events began to press heavily upon Tessa's shoulders, the adrenaline that had fueled her now dissipating like mist in the gathering dusk.

"Elle, I think you were right," Tessa finally admitted, "I'm sorry, but I need to turn in early." There was a hint of apology in her voice, a silent plea for understanding that she knew Elle would give without hesitation.

"Of course, Tess," Elle said warmly, her concern evident. "You've been through the wringer. Go get some rest; I'll clean up here."

"Thank you." Tessa stood, her movements slow, every muscle protesting the day's relentless pace. "Make yourself at home, okay? There's coffee for the morning, and help yourself to anything in the fridge."

"Will do," Elle assured her, a comforting presence in the encroaching night. "Sleep well."

Tessa nodded, managing a weary but genuine smile, before heading inside. She paused at the door, glancing back at the silhouette of her friend and mentor outlined against the backdrop of the ever-darkening sky. There was solace in knowing Elle was there—a guard of sorts in the quiet hours of the night.

With heavy steps, Tessa made her way to her bedroom, the soft creaks of the wooden floorboards beneath her feet a stark reminder of the solitude that awaited her. The bed seemed to beckon, promising oblivion from the ceaseless churn of her mind. She slipped under the covers without bothering to change, letting the darkness envelop her.

She was asleep in just a few breaths.

***

Sunlight pierced the gap between the drapes, casting a golden stripe across the foot of Tessa's bed. Her eyelids fluttered open, responding to the intrusion of morning with reluctance. The world was quiet, too quiet, and it nudged at her consciousness that something was amiss. Blinking the sleep from her eyes, pushed herself upright against the pillows, muscles stiff from the previous day's exertions. The clock on the bedside table read just past seven—a lie-in, by her standards. Rubbing at her temples, where a dull ache had taken residence, she let out a deep breath and swung her legs over the side of the bed.

Padding softly down the hallway, her bare feet whispered across the cool wooden planks. The door to the guestroom was ajar, and Tessa peered inside to find the room empty. The bed was made neatly, the sheets tucked in tight. A pang of disappointment tugged at her; she had hoped to continue their conversation from last night over a strong cup of coffee.

As she reached the kitchen, Tessa spotted an envelope resting on the counter, her name scrawled across it in Elle's familiar, assertive hand. Beside it lay a note, weighted down by a ceramic coffee mug. She picked up the note first, scanning the words quickly.

Thank you for the hospitality, Tess. Sorry to leave so early—duty calls. We'll catch up properly tonight. I should be back by 6. Elle.

Tessa's gaze shifted to the envelope, its contents a mystery that gnawed at her curiosity. With a sense of ritual, she slid her finger under the sealed flap and tore it open, the paper yielding to her touch with a soft rip that seemed louder than it should have in the silence of the kitchen.

Inside, she found a stack of documents, official-looking with the creases worn soft from frequent handling. The header of the top page bore the insignia of the Federal Bureau of Investigation, and below it, a name that sent a jolt through Tessa's chest.

Sarah Flint.

Her fingers tightened around the papers as she pulled them free from their confines, the action stirring a flurry of dust motes in the sunbeam. It was her sister's case file, the one that had gone cold six years ago. That stubborn ember of hope, never quite extinguished in Tessa's heart, flared to life. Tears formed in her eyes, and her body felt both hot and cold all at once.

Tucked within the pages was another note, this one shorter and carrying the weight of unsaid things:

Tess, I poked around a bit and I don't know if the department heads will let you look into this officially. But here's the official file to get YOU started. Just be careful. Elle.

Breath catching in her throat, Tessa spread the documents across the kitchen table, her eyes scanning the text for anything she might have missed all those years ago. Elle's gift was a tangible link to the sister she'd lost, a path shrouded in shadows but now handed to her with trust and friendship.

She already had most of the documents in digital form—files she'd managed to save and scavenge in private over the past year or so. But there were also some new things…several pages she'd not yet seen, details unread.

The quiet of the morning enveloped Tessa as she leaned over the report, every word, every detail, a whisper from the past calling her to unravel its secrets. The Hutch Pearson case head was forgotten, the fatigue that clung to her limbs cast aside. There was work to be done, and for the first time in a long while, Tessa felt the stirrings of a purpose that went beyond duty—it was personal.

See carried the folder and files out onto the back porch with a cup of coffee. The brisk morning air bit at her skin. The world around her was still, the sea beyond her backyard a sheet of glass reflecting the waking sky. Her eyes, though heavy with the remnants of yesterday's toil, were bright with determination. She flipped open Sarah's file, her fingers tracing the edges of the paper as if to draw strength from the fibers.

Photographs spilled out onto her lap, images of the life Sarah once had—a life cut tragically short. Tessa's gaze lingered on her sister's smile, preserved in the grainy black and white of police photography. It was a smile that never reached the eyes, a harbinger of the darkness that would soon engulf their lives. For a moment, Tessa allowed herself to feel the full weight of her loss, a luxury she seldom afforded herself. But there was no time for grief, not now, not when answers might lay hidden among these pages.

As Tessa pored over the report, each word etched itself into her memory. The initial call, the arrival of first responders, the interviews with potential witnesses—she absorbed them all, searching for discrepancies, for missed connections. Her mind, trained to dissect and analyze, whirred into action, filtering through years of investigative debris to find the nugget of truth buried beneath. She saw the window, the busted screen in the lawn, and her sister's empty bed.

She could almost hear Elle's voice, steady and sure, reminding her to look at the evidence without bias, to piece together the puzzle without letting emotion cloud her judgment. But God, it was so hard to do when it was *Sarah.*

The sun climbed higher, casting light upon the words that danced before Tessa's eyes. A statement out of place, a timeline that didn't add up, a piece of evidence overlooked—the possibilities began to form a map in her mind, leading her down a path she knew she must tread. This was more than just another case; it was a chance to right a wrong, to bring closure to a wound that had never truly healed.

Tessa Flint was no stranger to the dark alleys of human depravity she navigated in her line of work. But this...this was personal. This was for Sarah. With each turned page, Tessa felt the fire of resolve burn brighter within her. She would follow this trail wherever it led, even if it meant stepping outside the lines, even if it meant confronting her own demons along the way.

The ominous silence of the morning seemed to watch her, offering a challenge of sorts. And Tessa, with the files spread out like a challenge before her, did not hesitate to accept.

NOW AVAILABLE!

BARELY FORGOTTEN
(A Tessa Flint FBI Suspense Thriller—Book 3)

When a new serial killer targets victims in pitch-black rooms, their bodies marked with a hidden clue, FBI Agent Tessa Flint must delve into both the darkness of a killer's mind, and literal darkness, if she is to save the next victim in time…

"Molly Black has written a taut thriller that will keep you on the edge of your seat… I absolutely loved this book and can't wait to read the next book in the series!"
—Reader review for Girl One: Murder

BARELY FORGOTTEN is BOOK #3 of a brand-new series by critically acclaimed and #1 bestselling mystery and suspense author Molly Black, whose books have received over 2,000 five-star reviews and ratings. The series begins with BARELY SEEN (book #1).

The Tessa Flint series is an intense and riveting crime thriller that centers around a captivating and deeply troubled female protagonist. This gripping mystery series is filled with constant action, suspense, unexpected surprises, shocking discoveries, and propelled by a relentless speed that will have you engrossed in the story long into the night. Fans of Lisa Gardner, Teresa Driscoll and Karin Slaughter are sure to fall in love.

Future books in the series are also available.

"I binge read this book. It hooked me in and didn't stop till the last few pages… I look forward to reading more!"
—Reader review for Found You

"I loved this book! Fast-paced plot, great characters and interesting insights into investigating cold cases. I can't wait to read the next book!"
—Reader review for Girl One: Murder

"Very good book… You will feel like you are right there looking for the kidnapper! I know I will be reading more in this series!"
—Reader review for Girl One: Murder

"This is a very well written book and holds your interest from page 1… Definitely looking forward to reading the next one in the series, and hopefully others as well!"
—Reader review for Girl One: Murder

"Wow, I cannot wait for the next in this series. Starts with a bang and just keeps going."
—Reader review for Girl One: Murder

"Well written book with a great plot, one that will keep you up at night. A page turner!"
—Reader review for Girl One: Murder

"A great suspense that keeps you reading… can't wait for the next in this series!"
—Reader review for Found You

"Sooo soo good! There are a few unforeseen twists… I binge read this like I binge watch Netflix. It just sucks you in."
—Reader review for Found You

Molly Black

Bestselling author Molly Black is author of the MAYA GRAY FBI suspense thriller series, comprising ten books (and counting); of the RYLIE WOLF FBI suspense thriller series, comprising six books; of the TAYLOR SAGE FBI suspense thriller series, comprising eight books; of the KATIE WINTER FBI suspense thriller series, comprising eleven books (and counting); of the RUBY HUNTER FBI suspense thriller series, comprising five books (and counting); of the CAITLIN DARE FBI suspense thriller series, comprising six books (and counting); of the REESE LINK mystery series, comprising six books (and counting); of the CLAIRE KING FBI suspense thriller series, comprising seven books (and counting); of the PIPER WOODS mystery series, comprising five books (and counting); of the GRACE FORD mystery series, comprising seven books (and counting); of the CASEY BOLT mystery series, comprising five books (and counting); of the JADE SAVAGE mystery series, comprising five books (and counting); and of the TESSA FLINT mystery series, comprising five books (and counting).

An avid reader and lifelong fan of the mystery and thriller genres, Molly loves to hear from you, so please feel free to visit www.mollyblackauthor.com to learn more and stay in touch.

BOOKS BY MOLLY BLACK

TESSA FLINT MYSTERY SERIES
BARELY SEEN (Book #1)
BARELY HEARD (Book #2)
BARELY FORGOTTEN (Book #3)
BARELY MISSING (Book #4)
BARELY ALIVE (Book #5)

JADE SAVAGE MYSTERY SERIES
ALL SHE FEARS (Book #1)
ALL SHE WANTS (Book #2)
ALL SHE REMEMBERS (Book #3)
ALL SHE NEEDS (Book #4)
ALL SHE HIDES (Book #5)

CASEY BOLT MYSTERY SERIES
BROKEN (Book #1)
FLAWED (Book #2)
BLEMISHED (Book #3)
DAMAGED (Book #4)
TWISTED (Book #5)

GRACE FORD MYSTERY SERIES
NEARLY MINE (Book #1)
NEARLY SAFE (Book #2)
NEARLY FREE (Book #3)
NEARLY GONE (Book #4)
NEARLY HIS (Book #5)

CLAIRE KING MYSTERY SERIES
ONCE HE SEES (Book #1)
ONCE HE LONGS (Book #2)
ONCE HE TAKES (Book #3)
ONCE HE FEELS (Book #4)
ONCE HE KNOWS (Book #5)

MAYA GRAY MYSTERY SERIES
GIRL ONE: MURDER (Book #1)
GIRL TWO: TAKEN (Book #2)
GIRL THREE: TRAPPED (Book #3)
GIRL FOUR: LURED (Book #4)
GIRL FIVE: BOUND (Book #5)
GIRL SIX: FORSAKEN (Book #6)
GIRL SEVEN: CRAVED (Book #7)
GIRL EIGHT: HUNTED (Book #8)
GIRL NINE: GONE (Book #9)

RYLIE WOLF FBI SUSPENSE THRILLER
FOUND YOU (Book #1)
CAUGHT YOU (Book #2)
SEE YOU (Book #3)
WANT YOU (Book #4)
TAKE YOU (Book #5)
DARE YOU (Book #6)

TAYLOR SAGE FBI SUSPENSE THRILLER
DON'T LOOK (Book #1)
DON'T BREATHE (Book #2)
DON'T RUN (Book #3)
DON'T FLINCH (Book #4)
DON'T REMEMBER (Book #5)
DON'T TELL (Book #6)

KATIE WINTER FBI SUSPENSE THRILLER
SAVE ME (Book #1)
REACH ME (Book #2)
HIDE ME (Book #3)
BELIEVE ME (Book #4)
HELP ME (Book #5)
FORGET ME (Book #6)
HOLD ME (Book #7)
PROTECT ME (Book #8)
REMEMBER ME (Book #9)
CATCH ME (Book #10)
WATCH ME (Book #11)

RUBY HUNTER FBI SUSPENSE THRILLER
IF I RUN (Book #1)
IF I TELL (Book #2)
IF I LIVE (Book #3)
IF I FORGET (Book #4)
IF I RETURN (Book #5)

CAITLIN DARE FBI SUSPENSE THRILLER
COME GET ME (Book #1)
COME FIND ME (Book #2)
COME TAKE ME (Book #3)
COME CATCH ME (Book #4)
COME SAVE ME (Book #5)

REESE LINK MYSTERY
BEYOND REASON (Book #1)
BEYOND REACH (Book #2)
BEYOND REPAIR (Book #3)
BEYOND DOUBT (Book #4)
BEYOND NORMAL (Book #5)

Printed in Great Britain
by Amazon

54240839R00088